THE AGE OF THE ELEMENTS

Chapter I: Dawn of the Elements

At the dawn of time, the world lay in pristine stillness, a vast unpainted canvas, awaiting the brushstrokes of fate. It was an era of silence, where earth, water, air and fire existed in a state of precarious balance, without direction or purpose. This was the infancy of the world, a period marked by the absence of life and movement, a stillness that preceded the storm of creation.

From the depths of the cosmos, a spark emerged, a whisper of energy that began to weave the fabric of destiny. It was then that the Six Dragons emerged, born from the very essence of the elements they would govern. They were not mere creatures, but incarnations of the primordial forces of the world, each a guardian of the pillars on which reality would rest.

These colossal beings, still nameless in the world's memory, awoke to a solitary existence, each in a different corner of the vast void. With his arrival, the world began to take shape; Mountains arose with their roars, oceans were formed with their breath, and the skies cleared in their wake. However, in their immensity and power, they found rivalry among themselves. Each dragon, driven by an innate instinct to dominate, sought supremacy over others, wishing to impose order and structure according to its own vision.

The struggle for dominance was not merely physical, but a battle of wills, a dance of power that resonated across the vast plains and highest peaks. The elements, under his command, collided in spectacles of beauty and terror, sculpting the world in his image. Fire against water, earth against air, light against darkness; Each confrontation was a brushstroke on the canvas of reality, defining the borders of the nascent world.

Still, in the midst of this primordial chaos, there was a purpose. With each battle, the world became richer, more diverse. The dragons, in their eternal conflict, did not realize that they were contributing to the creation of a world where life could eventually flourish. Their confrontations, while destructive, also carried with them the seeds of creation, shaping the world into a place of infinite possibilities.

The Six Dragons remained nameless, titanic and mysterious figures whose true natures and powers were yet to be revealed. Their stories, woven into the very fabric of the world, were just beginning to unfold. This was the beginning of it all, a time before time, where the foundations of the world were established in a symphony of chaos and harmony.

Thus, in the infancy of the world, the Six Dragons emerged as the first and most powerful inhabitants, destined to rule and shape the elements. Their legacy would be eternal, their stories etched in the world's memory, waiting to be discovered and told in the ages to come.

In the heart of a still young world, where the elements intertwined in an eternal dance of creation and destruction, an imposing figure emerged, dominated by flame and wrath. This was "The Wild One", the first among the Six Dragons, whose birth was announced with a volcano awakening from its ancient slumber. His body, covered in scales that glowed like embers in the midday sun, stood majestically above the landscape, a living testament to the uncontrollable power of fire.

"The Wild One" was not named that on a whim. His temper, as fierce and unpredictable as the fire he commanded, manifested itself in every spark of his being. The forests turned to ashes in their wake, and the mountains trembled before their fury. However, his power did not lie solely in destruction. With every fire, with every flare that consumed the land, "The Wild One" brought renewal. The ashes fertilized the soil, giving way to new growth, new beginnings. It was the eternal cycle of destruction and rebirth, ruled by the indomitable hand of the fire dragon.

The legend of "The Wild One" began to take shape when, for the first time, he challenged the heavens. In an act of absolute defiance, he ascended into the infinite blue, his spread wings cutting through the clouds, his incendiary breath defying the sun. It was then that the world, in a collective whisper of wonder and awe, bestowed upon him his name. It was not only his indomitable nature that inspired both fear and admiration, but his iron will to assert his dominance over the element he ruled.

But "The Wild One" was not a creature without purpose or conscience. In his own way, he sought to understand the extent of his power and the role he must play in the balance of the world. His travels took him to the remotest reaches of the world, where flames danced in harmony with life. He observed how the smallest creatures depended on heat to survive and how fire, in its essence, was both a destroyer and a creator. In these moments of contemplation, "The Wild One" began to glimpse a deeper truth about his existence and the delicate balance he must maintain.

Despite his fiery nature, "The Wild One" was also a guardian. Their fire, although destructive, was essential to life and growth. Thus, he began to shape the world in his image, not only through devastation, but also allowing life to blossom from the ashes. It created vast plains and deep valleys, where natural fire cleansed and renewed, where new species could thrive.

In his solitude, "The Wild One" became a legend, a being feared and revered. His name was whispered with a mixture of fear and respect, a warning and a blessing. Although the other dragons emerged, each with their own dominion and power, "The Wild One" stood apart, a lone firelord whose breath could set entire forests ablaze and whose fury was as intense as the sun itself.

Thus, the saga of "The Wild One" was woven into the tapestry of the world, a story of power, passion, and the eternal cycle of destruction and rebirth. His legacy, forged in flame and ash, would be a perennial reminder that even in the heart of the most devastating fire, lies the seed of new life.

At a time when the world was still searching for its definitive form, an entity of incomparable power and serenity emerged from the ocean depths. This was "The Pacific", whose mere presence brought calm to the most turbulent waters. With scales that reflected the vastness of the sky and the depth of the sea, she glided across the oceans with a grace that belied her immense power. "The Pacific" was a balanced incarnate, the mediator between the fury of the sea and the tranquility of the depths.

From the beginning, "The Pacific" understood the duality of its domain. The waters of the world, capable of nourishing life and at the same time unleashing unparalleled fury, were a reflection of his own essence. He could raise gigantic waves and summon storms that rivaled the wrath of "The Wild One", but he chose to do so only when necessary, to maintain balance and teach the creatures of the world respect for the power of water.

The name "The Pacific" was bestowed upon him not because of his reluctance to show his power, but because of his preference for harmony and balance over conflict. Although he could unleash massive storms on the oceans, he did so for the purpose of cleansing and renewal, of bringing fresh water to thirsty lands and of guiding lost travelers to safety. His wisdom was as deep as the ocean abysses, and all beings who lived in the water saw him as their protector and guide.

"The Pacific" also played a crucial role in the eternal dance of creation and destruction that defined the world. Through its tides, it shaped the coasts and beaches, shaped the continents and regulated the climate. Their influence extended beyond the limits of water, affecting land and air, and demonstrating how the elements were intrinsically connected.

However, despite his immense power, "The Pacific" was a creature of deep introspection. In the darkest depths, where sunlight could not reach, he meditated on the nature of balance and the interconnectedness of all things. He understood that his strength lay not in domination, but in the ability to unite and sustain life in all its forms.

Occasionally, "The Pacific" would emerge from his seclusion to meet the other dragons, sharing his vision of a harmonious world. Although their encounters were rare, they left a lasting impression, reminding other dragons of the importance of balance and peaceful coexistence.

Over time, the name "The Pacific" became synonymous with wisdom, serenity and the irrepressible power of the sea. His legacy was interwoven with the myths and legends of sailors and coastal people, stories of a dragon whose breath could calm the fiercest storms and whose scales shone with the reflection of the calm ocean.

Thus, in the pages of world history, "The Pacific" stood as the undisputed guardian of the waters, a beacon of calm in a world of constant changes and challenges. Its influence spread across all seas and rivers, an eternal reminder of the power that lies in peace and balance.

In a world still in formation, where the fire burned with fury and the waters whispered of calm and storm, a presence arose as volatile as the air itself. This was "The Changeling", the third dragon, whose essence was intertwined with the wind and the sky. There was no mountain so high or valley so deep that could escape his reach. Its wings, immense as the horizon, shook the heavens, summoning whirlwinds and hurricanes that could destroy everything in its path.

"The Changeling" did not receive its name by chance. Among all dragons, he possessed a singularity that set him apart: the ability to change shape at will. This ability not only made him an unpredictable force on the battlefield, but also allowed him to walk among the creatures of the world in any way he desired. It could be as gentle as a spring breeze that caresses the skin or as devastating as a tornado that leaves nothing in its wake.

The nature of "The Changeling" was as varied as the wind he governed. It could be seen as a harbinger of change, carrying the seeds of renewal wherever its storms touched the earth. Under his care, the cycles of nature flowed unimpeded, as the wind was essential for spreading pollen, refreshing stagnant waters, and purifying the air. In this regard, "The Changeling" was both creator and destroyer, a guardian of the world's natural balance.

Despite his formidable power and capricious nature, "The Changeling" was a being of deep thoughts and reflections. His ability to assume any form gave him a unique perspective on life in the world. He saw the world through the eyes of countless creatures, understanding their fears, their hopes, and their dreams. This empathy, born of his mutability, made him a wise mediator between dragons, able to understand and value the differences that often brought them into conflict.

However, its unpredictability also instilled fear in those who did not understand its true nature. Mortal beings saw in "The Changeling" a figure of mystery and unfathomable power, a being whose actions could bring blessings as well as calamities. The legends about him were as many as the forms he could take, narratives that spoke of a free spirit that could not be tied to any form or destiny.

The abode of "The Changeling" was not fixed in any place. He could be found on the summit of the highest mountain, where the air was so thin that one could barely breathe, or wandering the vast plains, where the wind whispered ancient secrets. He was often seen riding the air currents, observing from above the world that constantly changed under his influence.

In the history of the world, "The Changeling" would stand as the spirit of the wind incarnate, a perpetual reminder that change is eternal and necessary. His legacy would be one of transformation and adaptability, teaching all creatures that, like the wind, they must be willing to change, to flow and adapt to the ever-changing whims of life.

In an era marked by tumult and transformation, where the skies and seas heaved under the power of dragons, the land itself found its defender. This was "The Firm One", the fourth of the Six Dragons, whose essence was intertwined with the stone, mineral and fertile soil of the nascent world. His imposing figure, covered in scales that emulated the hardest and oldest rocks, stood as a monument to the immutable force of the earth.

"The Firm One" not only possessed the firmness and stability of the land he ruled; His breath, capable of shaking the foundations of the world, could summon devastating earthquakes, opening cracks in the surface of the planet that swallowed entire cities. However, despite his destructive power, "The Firm One" was a creator, a shaper of mountains and valleys, an architect of the geography of the world.

The name "The Firm One" was derived not only from his dominance over the land, but also from his unwavering determination and indomitable character. It was the pillar on which the other elements rested, the foundation that supported the balance of the world. Their presence inspired a sense of security and permanence, a reminder that, despite storms and fires, the land would remain.

His kingdom was vast, ranging from the highest, snow-capped, heaven-defying mountains to the hidden depths beneath the surface, where ancient secrets and precious minerals lay. "The Firm One" knew every crevice and cave, every corner of his domain, and guarded it jealousy, ensuring that the life that flourished on and within the land was protected and nurtured.

Despite his imposing appearance and his ability to cause natural catastrophes, "The Firm One" was a dragon with a gentle heart. His connection with the earth gave him a deep empathy towards all the creatures that lived on it. He knew the cycle of life and death, the importance of renewal and regeneration. The earthquakes and the eruptions they caused were, in his vision, ways to revitalize the world, to bring new opportunities for growth and evolution.

"The Firm One" was also a guardian, watching out against those who would seek to unbalance the world for their own benefit. Its power was a deterrent against arrogance and excessive ambition, a reminder that the earth, while patient and generous, could also be relentless in its wrath.

In the tapestria of the world, the story of "The Firm One" was woven with threads of stability and strength, but also of change and renewal. His legacy was one of respect for the land and understanding of its fundamental importance in the balance of the world. Future generations would speak of him not only as the dragon who could shake the earth, but as the one who sustained it, nourished it, and protected it, a true Sovereign of the Earth.

In the primordial era, when the foundations of the world were still being forged under the influence of the elemental dragons, fate wove a new weave into the tapestry of creation. Emerging simultaneously from the ends of the cosmic spectrum, the last of the Six Dragons appeared: "The Glorious One" and "The Dark One", entities that embodied light and darkness, respectively. Their emergence marked a moment of profound change, because with them came the final balance between all the contrasts in the world.

"The Glorious One" was born from the first light of dawn, a being whose essence was pure radiation and radiance. Its scales shone with the intensity of a thousand suns, and its presence brought clarity to even the darkest nights. It was a dragon of magnificent beauty, whose spread wings dyed the sky with warm, golden tones, announcing the beginning of a new day. "The Glorious One" not only dispelled physical darkness, but also inspired hope and courage in the hearts of all creatures, a beacon of certainty in times of doubt.

On the other hand, "The Dark One" emerged from the depths of the most impenetrable night, an entity shrouded in shadows and mystery. His figure, although slender and elegant, was perpetually covered by a haze of darkness that hid his true form from curious eyes. "The Dark One" was the lord of all that was hidden and unknown, ruling over the secrets that were hidden in the shadows. Despite his intimidating appearance and the fear his name inspired, "The Dark One" protected the mysteries of the world and maintained the balance between the visible and the invisible.

The simultaneous appearance of "The Glorious One" and "The Dark One" was not a coincidence, but a design of fate. They were two sides of the same coin, the opposite but complementary forces that maintained the balance of the universe. Together, they represented the duality inherent in all existence: light and darkness, day and night, revelation and enigma. Although different in nature and purpose, both dragons were essential to the harmony of the world.

Their relationship was complex, marked by mutual understanding and deep respect for the role each played. "The Glorious One" and "The Dark One" rarely faced each other directly, aware that their fight could trigger a catastrophic imbalance. Instead, they chose to coexist, their influences intertwining in an eternal cycle that defined the passage of time and the seasons.

Over the ages, "The Glorious One" and "The Dark One" became legendary figures, revered and feared in equal measure by the civilizations that arose under their watch. Temples were erected in their honor, and their stories were told in myths and legends, narratives that sought to explain the constant presence of light and shadow in the world.

Thus, in the creation chapter, "The Glorious One" and "The Dark One" were established as the final guardians of duality, a perpetual reminder that neither light nor darkness can exist without the other. His legacy would be a testament to the complexity of the world, a world where light guides and darkness protects, maintaining the precious balance that allows all life to exist.

As eons gave way to eras, the world, still young and moldable, became the scene of unprecedented conflict. The Six Dragons, each a colossus of unimaginable power, engaged in an endless war for supremacy. These battles, titanic in scale and devastating in consequence, set the pace of existence for all creatures who dared to inhabit the world.

The heavens, a canvas of celestial serenity, were torn apart by the roar of their confrontations. "The Changeling", lord of the wind, summoned hurricanes that uprooted trees from their roots and diverted rivers from their courses. "The Firm One", guardian of the earth, responded with earthquakes that fractured continents, creating abysses where there once were plains.

From the ocean depths, "The Pacific" raised gigantic waves, tsunamis capable of engulfing entire cities in an instant. In contrast, "The Wild One" set fire to forests and meadows, his fiery breath turning the night into a simulacrum of the brightest day.

Meanwhile, in the eternal play of shadows and light, "The Dark One" and "The Glorious One" wove their power into the very fabric of reality. "The Glorious One" illuminated the skies with auroras that told stories of hope, while "The Dark One" enveloped the world in darkness, whispering forgotten secrets into the ear of the night.

These confrontations were not mere shows of force; They were cataclysms that reshaped the world. Mountains emerged from nowhere, islands sank into the sea abyss, and rivers changed their course, redrawing the map of the world with each encounter. The land itself bore the scars of their struggle, silent testimony of their battle for dominance.

Mortals, mere shadows under the magnitude of these beings, lived in a state of fear and amazement. Entire civilizations rose and fell at the whim of dragons. Although some learned to worship them as gods, offering sacrifices and prayers to appease their fury or gain their favor, others sought to hide, hoping to survive another day under the yoke of their endless war.

Nature itself seemed to beg for respite, longing for the peace it once knew before the heavens and earth were rent asunder by the clamor of battle. But the war between the dragons knew no end; His desire for supremacy was insatiable, and the world, his arena, was condemned to a perpetual cycle of creation and destruction.

In this endless chaos, the world teetered on the edge of the abyss. The constant struggle for power between the Six Dragons left little room for hope for an era of peace. Earth, air, fire, water, light and darkness; All the elements were in disarray, reflecting the tumult of their guardians.

Thus, in an era defined by conflict and uncertainty, the world waited, longing for the emergence of a new order that could bring harmony to the land. But until then, he would remain trapped in the whirlwind of eternal war, a perpetual chaos from which there seemed no escape.

As the world struggled in the grip of disorder, its lands torn by war and its skies darkened by smoke and storms, a change was brewing in the depths of despair. The incessant conflict between the dragons had brought the world to the brink of ruin. Rivers of lava flowed through what were once fertile valleys, and entire mountains had been displaced, leaving behind a trail of desolation and loss.

In this scenario of hopelessness, two figures emerged as bearers of a new future. "The Glorious One" and "The Dark One", eternal adversaries whose forces seemed to perpetuate the cycle of conflict, came to an understanding that would change the fate of the world. Tired of a struggle that seemed to consume not only their energies but the very fabric of creation, they decided to look for a solution that until then seemed impossible.

Their meeting took place in a forgotten corner of the world, a place where the light of day and the shadows of night intertwine in an eternal twilight, symbolizing the union of their essences. This place, hidden from the eyes of mortals and other dragons, would serve as a witness to the birth of a new era.

The meeting between "The Glorious One" and "The Dark One" was a spectacle of power and delicacy, a perfect balance between light and darkness. As they approached, their opposing energies began to resonate, creating an aura of power that illuminated the sky with colors never seen before. The earth trembled, not in fear, but as if in anticipation of the birth of a new hope.

In that sacred moment, "The Glorious One" spread his resplendent wing, while "The Dark One" wrapped his shadowy essence around them both. The words they exchanged were more than promises; They were vows of a new beginning, a commitment to end the war and rule together, merging their forces to restore balance to the world.

The pact they made was sealed with a light that penetrated the shadows, and a darkness that embraced every brightness, symbolizing their indissoluble union. They swore before the primordial forces of the universe, pledging to unite their powers not to dominate, but to protect and revitalize the world they had torn apart with their conflicts.

This meeting, marked by solemnity and hope, promised a new era of peace and harmony. The other dragons, sensing the change in the air, looked towards the place of the pact in awe and dawning hope. Perhaps, for the first time in countless cycles, the world would have a chance to heal and flourish under the guidance of these two transformed beings.

Thus, in the union of "The Glorious One" and "The Dark One", the key to peace was found. Their pact not only symbolized the end of their rivalry, but also the beginning of a new alliance that would lead the world out of the shadows of chaos and into the light of a new day.

The union of "The Glorious One" and "The Dark One" marked a turning point in the history of the world. The fusion of light and darkness, two forces that had been considered eternally opposed, created a spectacle of unparalleled beauty, a mystical glow that illuminated the sky while casting dancing shadows across the earth. This never-before-seen phenomenon served as a beacon of change, a harbinger of a new era of balance and harmony.

The reaction of the other four dragons to this union was one of amazement and revelation. "The Wild One", whose flames had consumed countless forests in his quest for supremacy, was captivated by the serenity that emanated from the glow. Its flames, for the first time, burned not with fury, but with a warmth that embraced life rather than destroying it.

"The Pacific", whose tides had shaped coasts and drowned lands in their expression of power, found in the combined aura a depth greater than that of any ocean. The waters of the world, reflecting the enchanted sky, calmed, as if understanding that true strength lay in the ability to unite and sustain, not divide and destroy.

"The Changeling", master of the wind, whose currents had carried out the will to change with a sometimes destructive intensity, felt the air filled with a new promise. The winds that blew that day did not speak of storms, but of messages of peace, carrying the news of the union to all corners of the world.

Finally, "The Firm One" whose connection to the earth had caused earthquakes and forged mountains in his display of power, perceived a new kind of strength in the balance achieved by "The Glorious One" and "The Dark One". The earth beneath his feet, always his domain, resonated with a pulse of rejuvenated life, reminding him that true solidity comes from harmony, not division.

The astonishing display of power and unity between "The Glorious one" and "The Dark One" was enough to cause the other dragons to cease their hostilities. They understood, perhaps for the first time, that their endless war had been nothing more than a barrier to their world's true potential. Peace, they realized, was not simply the absence of conflict, but the presence of a balance in which all elements could coexist and thrive.

With this new understanding, the Six Dragons gathered, not as adversaries, but as custodians of a world they had sworn to protect. Together, they forged a pact, inspired by the example of "The Glorious One" and "The Dark One", pledging to rule in harmony and to use their power not to dominate one another, but to sustain and enrich life in all its forms.

Thus, the great war between the dragons came to an end. The world, which had trembled under the yoke of their conflict, began to heal. The scars of past battles became reminders of the importance of balance and unity. Under the guidance of the Six Dragons, a new era of prosperity and peace swept the world, a living testament to the transformative power of harmony.

The culmination of the war between the dragons and the formation of their pact of unity marked the beginning of a new era for the world. For the first time in history, the Six Dragons, once adversaries in an endless struggle for supremacy, came together for a common purpose: to safeguard the harmony of the world they had shaped and often disfigured with their conflicts. Recognizing the strength inherent in the union of darkness and light, they established a new order based on cooperation and mutual respect.

Under this new order, dragons took on roles not as tyrannical rulers, but as protectors and guardians. The task they set for themselves was monumental: maintaining the balance of the elements, ensuring that none predominated over the others, so that life in all its forms could thrive. "The Glorious One" and "The Dark One", whose alliance had been the catalyst for this change, led the effort, serving as living examples of the power that lies in the harmony of opposites.

"The Wild One", with his mastery over fire, took on the responsibility of renewing and purifying, using his flames not for destruction, but to encourage growth and regeneration. "The

Pacific", lord of the waters, guaranteed that rivers and seas nourished the land, and that the rains arrived in time for the harvests, blessing the world with its generosity.

"The Changeling", master of the wind, became the messenger between the elements, carrying seeds, clouds and scents across vast distances, linking the world with invisible currents of connection. "The Firm One", ruler of the earth, stabilized the world, ensuring that the earth was fertile and solid, a safe home for the countless life forms that walked upon it.

This new order brought with it lasting peace. Mortals, who once lived under the shadow of fear and uncertainty, were now flourishing. Entire civilizations were built under the protection of dragons, and the wisdom of these immortal beings was freely shared with those who sought to understand the mysteries of the world.

The dragons, in turn, found renewed purpose in their role as guardians. Through collaboration, they learned from each other, appreciating the differences that had previously divided them.

Humility replaced pride, and mutual respect forged an indestructible bond between them.

In their wisdom, the Six Dragons understood that balance was a continuous process, a task that would require their constant vigilance. Nature's cycles, seasons and climatic changes were now carefully moderated, keeping the world in a harmony that allowed all life to thrive. Natural disasters, when they occurred, were less destructive and served as reminders of the strength of nature and the need to live in respect for the world.

Thus, dragons became more than mere rulers or warriors; They stood as pillars of the world, custodians of life and architects of a future where all beings could coexist in peace. The Age of the Guardians had begun, a testament to the transformative power of balance and unity.

The era of peace and balance, ushered in by the Six Dragons alliance, marked the dawn of a new chapter in the history of the world. The union between the Glorious and the Dark One, a time unthinkable, became the beacon of hope that guided all creatures toward a future of harmony. However, as with all light, the shadows persisted, subtle but present, reminding everyone that peace is a delicate state, constantly in need of care and protection.

Despite the prevailing tranquility, the world faced new challenges. The concentration of the population in a single large settlement began to generate tensions, both in terms of resources and space. Humanity, relieved from the constant threat of dragon warfare, began to explore its own ambitions, sometimes forgetting the lessons of balance and unity that dragons strove to teach.

The Six Dragons, aware of these growing problems, knew that their mission went beyond simply protecting the natural world. It was necessary to guide future generations, teaching them to live in harmony not only with the world around them but also with each other. Thus, they began to disperse, each one bringing their wisdom to different corners of the world, inspiring communities to settle far from the original settlement, promoting diversity and self-sufficiency.

"The Wild One", for example, led groups of humans into the vast plains and taught them the art of controlling fire, not for destruction, but for hunting, cooking food, and protection against wild beasts. "The Pacific" guided others to the coasts and rivers, showing them how to fish and use the water to irrigate their crops, thus ensuring their livelihood.

"The Changeling", loving freedom and exploration, inspired many to travel far, taking them across mountains and valleys, teaching them to read wind and weather patterns to navigate and discover new lands. "The Firm One", with his deep knowledge of the land, helped establish communities in mountainous and arid regions, instructing them in building stable dwellings and extracting minerals and resources from the soil.

This dispersal of humanity not only eased tensions over resources but also fostered the rise of diverse cultures and civilizations, each adapting and thriving in their unique environment under the tutelage of the dragons. The teachings of the Six Dragons were woven into the culture and traditions of these new societies, reminding them of the importance of balance and peaceful coexistence.

However, even in this era of peace, the dragons knew they must remain vigilant. The harmony of the world depended on constant balance, and although they had guided humanity towards a brighter future, human nature was unpredictable. The shadows of ambition, fear and oblivion always lurked, threatening to unbalance the hard-won peace.

The Six Dragons, now seen not only as protectors but also as teachers and guides, continued their tireless work. Their presence was a constant reminder that peace is a garden that requires attention and care, and that each generation must work to preserve the balance, ensuring that the light of hope is never extinguished in the darkness of disunity.

Chapter II: The Council of Elements

At the dawn of an era of peace, with the alliance between light and darkness sealed, the Six Dragons gathered for a council unlike any other in history. This meeting, far from the shadows of past conflicts, was dedicated to dialogue and a shared vision of the future. Their mission was transcendental: to determine how the world would be divided among them, defining kingdoms where each dragon would exercise its tutelage over the elements and their creatures.

The location chosen for this monumental debate was as impressive as the participants: a floating island in the sky, where the infinite met the eternal. In this place, where the air danced with the clouds and the earth touched the firmament, the dragons gathered, each one embodying the essence and power of their element.

"The Wild One", with a voice that boomed like a burning fire, expressed his desire to reign over vast prairies and mountain ranges, domains where the heat of the sun would forge life and rebirth. His kingdom would be a testimony of strength and purification, a sanctuary where fire would sculpt nature.

"The Pacific", whose voice flowed like the waters it represents, aspired to rule over oceans, rivers and lagoons. Its domain

would be one of serenity and sustenance, in which the waters
would foster life and guide civilizations to prosperity and
well-being.

"The Changeling", with a voice that varied with the wind,
expressed his desire to influence the entire world without a fixed
kingdom, symbolizing the constant and vital presence of air for
life, communication and renewal.

"The Firm One", with a voice as robust as the earth itself,
declared his will to guard the vast mountains, valleys and
deserts. His kingdom promised stability and wealth, offering
fertile soils and mineral resources to support lasting civilizations.

In turn, "The Glorious One" and "The Dark One", in a duet of
voices that weaved light and shadow, revealed a renewed vision.
Unlike their brothers, they would not only seek to balance the
world from the shadows; each desired a kingdom of their own,
hidden from the sight of the others, from where they could
observe and protect the balance of all domains. The kingdom of
"The Glorious One" would be a sanctuary of eternal light,

accessible only through the purest of heart, a place of wisdom and healing. For his part, "The Dark One" would claim a domain shrouded in mystery and tranquility, a refuge for those who sought to understand the depths of existence away from the clamor of the world.

The debate that followed was as deep as the world itself. Each dragon contributed from their essence, intertwining their visions into a complex mosaic of possibilities for the future. They discussed the boundaries of their kingdoms, the interaction between their elements, and the ways in which they would protect and guide the creatures in their care.

This council was not intended to reach hasty resolutions. It was a conversation that demanded time, reflection and, above all, a commitment to the balance and unity that now defined their coexistence. The dragons understood that their decisions would echo through the ages, shaping the destiny of a world that had bordered on the abyss of destruction.

And so, amid fiery speeches and watery murmurs, earthly promises and wind-whispered secrets, with light and darkness in perfect harmony, the Six Dragons continued their deliberation. The story of their meeting would be inscribed in the memory of time, evidencing their dedication not only to their own domains but to the well-being of the cosmos as a whole.

In the golden age that followed the formation of the new dragon alliance, "The Glorious One" embarked on an unprecedented mission of creation. Moved by his essence of pure light and unwavering benevolence, he decided to forge a kingdom that would serve as a bastion of hope and guidance for all the creatures of the world. This kingdom would not have its place among the mountains nor along the vast oceans, but in the vast and infinite sky.

With a power that echoed the brilliance of dawn, "The Glorious one" summoned the forces of light and atmosphere to create an architectural marvel: a floating city that would rise above the clouds, a testament to the splendor and majesty. of his vision. This city, built with materials that reflected the light of the sun and stars, shone with a luminosity that could be seen from the most remote corners of the world. Its towers and bridges, bathed in the perpetual radiance of their creator, were a sight to behold, inspiring awe and admiration in all who looked up to the sky.

The City of Light, as it came to be known, was not just a visual marvel; It was a sanctuary of knowledge and wisdom. "The Glorious One" invited beings from all lands to become his subjects, offering them a home where darkness could never touch them, a place where eternal light promised safety and warmth. Here, scholars, artists, and dreamers of all races and species gathered, sharing their knowledge and discoveries, further enriching the culture and intellect of this celestial nation.

As time passed, the City of Light became a beacon of hope and a constant reminder of the presence and power of "The Glorious One." His light became a guide to lost sailors, a comfort to those suffering in darkness, and a symbol of what could be achieved when goodness and light prevailed over fear and darkness.

However, as the ages passed and generations of mortals gave way to the next, the physical presence of "The Glorious One" and his dragon brothers began to fade into the realm of legend. The dragons, once visible guardians and rulers of the world, chose to retreat from the sight of mortals, trusting the societies they had helped forge to continue their legacy of balance and harmony.

Although "The Glorious one" no longer walked among his subjects as before, his influence remained. The City of Light remained a testament to his existence and a reminder of the ideals he had imparted. The teachings and laws he established continued to guide the city, keeping the essence of its creator alive.

Today, the City of Light remains suspended in the sky, a mystery to many who only know its legend. It is said that on especially clear nights, its silhouette can be glimpsed against the starry sky, an eternal reminder that even in the deepest darkness, light can always find its way.

In contrast to the resplendent domain of his counterpart, "The Dark One" forged his kingdom far from the light of the sun, in an underground sanctuary where darkness reigned supreme. This realm, born from the very essence of night and mystery, became the heart of the depths of the earth, a labyrinth of caverns and halls carved into the living rock, where daylight could never penetrate.

The underground city, known as the Shelter of Shadows, was a marvel of ancient architecture and magic. Its hallways, illuminated only by crystals that captured the faint light of distant stars, snaked through the underground like rivers of shadow. Stalactites and stalagmites adorned its chambers like the jewels of a forgotten crown, creating a scene of unearthly beauty and quiet solemnity.

"The Dark One", in his infinite wisdom, conceived this kingdom not only as his abode but as a refuge for those who found in the darkness an ally rather than an enemy. Here, philosophers, alchemists, and occult scholars gathered, drawn by the promise of knowledge that could only be discovered far from the distraction of daylight. In the hidden libraries of the kingdom, hidden in silent caverns, tomes of ancient wisdom were accumulated, secrets of the universe waiting to be revealed to those brave enough to seek them.

Unlike the City of Light, which stood as a beacon to the outside world, the Haven of Shadows was an introspective sanctuary, a place of meditation and personal discovery. "The Dark One" taught that true understanding came from introspection and confronting one's own fears and doubts. Here, in the eternal gloom, individuals were invited to explore the depths of their being, finding in the darkness the clarity that the outside world could not offer.

As the centuries passed, the Shelter of Shadows became a center of learning like no other, a meeting point for those seeking answers to the deepest questions of existence. "The Dark One", although rarely shown in his true form, remained the silent guardian of this realm, ensuring that the accumulated knowledge was preserved and respected.

Like the City of Light, the Haven of Shadows went from a dominant physical presence to a whispered legend among those who sought truth in hidden places. It was said that its secret entrances could be found in the most remote corners of the world, waiting to be discovered by brave souls who were not afraid to venture into the darkness.

In the current era, where dragons have become figures of myth and legend, the Refuge of Shadows remains a symbol of the endless quest for knowledge and the realization that, in the depths of darkness, truths can be found that the brightest light cannot reveal.

Following the pact that ushered in an era of balance, "The Wild One", the dragon whose essence was intertwined with fire and renewal, chose the vast plains and towering erupting volcanoes as the foundation of his dominion. This kingdom, forged in the searing heat and dancing light of flames, became the home of those whose spirits burned with unwavering passion and bravery.

The Firelands, as they were known, were a spectacle of savage beauty and untamed power. Here, lava rivers snaked across the plains like veins of life, providing nutrients that enriched the land, allowing unique ecosystems resistant to extreme heat to flourish. Volcanoes, far from being seen as threats, were revered as sources of strength and renewal, each eruption a celebration of the creative energy of "The Wild One".

The inhabitants of these lands were as fierce and resilient as the environment in which they lived. Forged in the crucible of a fiery kingdom, they developed a society that valued boldness, fortitude, and the ability to thrive under adverse conditions. Hunting, agriculture, and crafts adapted to the peculiarities of their volcanic home, using heat and ash in innovative methods that were the envy of other nations.

"The Wild One" himself, although he rarely intervened directly in the affairs of his subjects, was a constant presence in their lives. Their fiery breath not only shaped the landscape, but also ignited in them the desire to constantly improve themselves, to face challenges with courage and to find in adversity the opportunity for personal and collective growth.

The culture that flourished in the Tierras de Fuego was imbued with a deep respect for the element that gave them life. Celebrations and rituals honoring "The Wild One" and fire were common, symbolizing both destruction and creation, the end and the new beginning. Artists and artisans created works that captured the essence of fire, from glass sculptures formed in extreme heat to fabrics dyed with the vibrant colors of flames.

Over time, and as generations passed, the physical presence of "The Wild One" faded into the mists of myth. Yet his legacy remained, rooted in the heart of his kingdom and its people. The Firelands continued to prosper, a living testament to the passion and resilience that "The Wild One" had inspired.

Today, the legends of "The Wild One" and his fiery kingdom persist, told around campfires and in the pages of history books. Although dragons no longer walk visibly among mortals, the spirit of "The Wild One" continues to burn in the souls of those who call the Firelands home, reminding them that even in the most devastating fire, there is a spark of opportunity for courage and renewal.

After the Six Dragons reached an agreement on the distribution of the world, "The Pacific", the guardian of the waters and tides, retreated to the vast blue expanses that cover much of the world. Here, in a domain where the horizon merges with the sky and the waves whisper ancient songs, he established his kingdom, a kingdom of islands scattered like jewels on the mantle of the ocean and of mysterious depths that hold ancient secrets.

This kingdom, known as the Kingdom of Still Waters, became a sanctuary of life and abundance. "The Pacific", with his deep knowledge of currents and tides, guided his subjects in the art of living in harmony with the sea. He taught them to read wave patterns, predict storms before they arose, and respect the waters that sustained them.

Under his tutelage, island societies flourished. The inhabitants of the Kingdom of Still Waters became sailors and navigators like no other, exploring the far reaches of the known world and beyond. Their ships, driven by the wind and current, sailed the seas in search of new lands, trade and knowledge. They became expert fishermen, whose nets always returned full, and astute traders, whose trade routes wove a web of connections between disparate cultures.

"The Pacific" also instilled in its people the importance of sustainability. He showed them how to harness the sea's resources without depleting them, how to protect the coral reefs that were the cradle of marine biodiversity, and how to ensure that future generations would inherit an ocean as rich and vibrant as the one they enjoyed. The fishing and navigation laws, dictated by "The Pacific", guaranteed that the balance between man and the sea was maintained.

Over time, the direct presence of "The Pacific" among his people faded, becoming a mythical figure, a spiritual protector who watched from the depths. However, his influence remained indelible in the maritime culture he had fostered. Festivals in their honor, filled with song and dance that imitated the flow of the tides, remained a central part of life in the Kingdom of Still Waters, and ancient teachings about harmony with the sea were passed down from generation to generation. .

In the current era, the Kingdom of Still Waters remains a place where the relationship with the ocean defines existence. The descendants of those first subjects of "The Pacific" continue to navigate the blue waters, trade with distant peoples and live off the generous gifts of the sea. The wisdom of "The Pacific" continues to guide them, an echo of its presence that reminds them of the importance of living in balance with the vast and mysterious aquatic world that surrounds them.

In the diverse fabric of the new world order established by the Six Dragons, "The Changeling" chose the vast grasslands, a domain as fluid and dynamic as his own nature. This kingdom, always moving under the command of the winds and the seasons, became home to a nomadic people, whose lives were intrinsically linked to the whims of the wind and the vast open sky.

These nomadic grasslands, stretching as far as the eye could see, were a mosaic of color and life. With each season, his appearance changed dramatically, reflecting the mutable nature of "The Changeling". In spring, they were dressed in vibrant green, dotted with wildflowers. In summer, golden waves of grass danced in the sun, while autumn turned the landscape red and bronze, preparing it for the white silence of winter.

The people of "The Changeling", like their patron, embraced the nomadic life with fervor and resilience. They were masters in the art of adapting, of understanding and predicting the changes in the wind that dictated the movement of their caravans. His tents, built to be set up and taken down quickly, were a testament to his ingenuity and commitment to a life in constant motion.

"The Changeling" taught his people to listen to the whispers of the wind, to interpret its messages and to follow its instructions to find water, shelter and pasture for their flocks. This deep understanding of the wind and its secrets not only ensured their survival, but also wove into the soul of their people the very essence of freedom and adaptability.

Over the generations, the nomadic grasslands became a melting pot of cultures and knowledge. Constant travel allowed the exchange of ideas and goods between different peoples, enriching nomadic society with a diversity that few kingdoms could match. The stories and legends of "The Changeling" and his teachings were passed around campfires under a starry sky, inspiring young and old alike to embrace change as an essential part of life.

Over time, the presence of "The Changeling" faded into the wind, leaving behind only the echo of his influence. However, his legacy lived on in the traditions and nomadic spirit of his people, who continued to wander the prairies, always in search of new horizons.

In the current era, the nomadic grasslands continue to be a place of life and movement. Although dragons have become figures of legends, the essence of "The Changeling" remains alive in the hearts of his descendants. In their adaptability, their respect for nature, and their love of freedom, the people of the nomadic grasslands continue to carry with them the essence of the wind, a constant reminder that, in change, lies the true essence of life.

In the new era of balance between the elements, "The Firm One", whose essence was deeply rooted in the solidity of the earth, chose the imposing mountain ranges and fertile valleys as the foundation of his kingdom. This domain, characterized by its unwavering stability and natural wealth, became the home of a people whose strength and resilience reflected the qualities of its guardian.

The mountains, rising majestically toward the heavens, were not mere natural barriers, but living fortresses that guarded ancient secrets and precious minerals within. The valleys, for their part, offered fertile lands bathed by crystalline rivers, where crops grew abundantly and life flourished in harmony with the rhythm of nature. "The Firm One" with his dominion over the land, shaped this landscape, creating safe havens and opportunities for prosperity for his subjects.

The people of "The Firm One" were characterized by their industrious spirit and tenacity. They were masters in the art of agriculture, cultivating the land with a deep respect for its cycles and its gifts. Mining, another of their great skills, allowed them to extract treasures hidden in the bowels of the earth, from precious metals to crystals of mystical power. However, despite their ability to take advantage of the earth's resources, they always did so with an awareness of their duty to protect and preserve the environment that "The Firm One" had entrusted to them.

The society that developed in this kingdom was based on collaboration and mutual respect. Building expertise, which used both stone and wood from the surrounding forests, ensured that each building was in harmony with the landscape, strengthening its connection to the land. The fortresses and villages stood as testimonies of their ability to work in conjunction with the environment, not against it.

As the generations passed, the direct presence of "The Firm One" faded in the collective memory, transforming into a mythical figure, the founder of their great civilization. However, the teachings and principles he had imparted remained alive in the traditions and daily practices of his people. Festivals celebrating the equinoxes and solstices, for example, were moments of deep spiritual connection with the land, reminders of the perpetual dance between man and nature.

Today, the descendants of those first inhabitants of the mountains and valleys continue to honor the legacy of "The Firm One". Their communities, despite the advances of the modern world, maintain a deep respect for the land that sustains them. The ancient rituals and legends of "The Firm One" remain an integral part of their identity, a moral compass that guides their interaction with the natural world.

Thus, the kingdom of "The Firm One" endures as a bastion of strength, work, and harmony with the land, a constant reminder that true wealth and security come from our unbreakable bond with the world around us.

In the intricate tapestry of the world, woven by the coexistence and contrasts of the elements, "The Glorious One" and "The Dark One" assumed essential roles as custodians of balance. Their alliance, once unthinkable, became the foundation upon which the harmony of the universe rested. From their unique abodes, they carefully watched the dance of creation, ensuring that the delicate balance that sustained life was not compromised.

"The Glorious One", residing above, in a sphere of eternal light near the sun, became the source of vital energy that nourished the vast kingdoms of his brothers. Its light, pure and revitalizing, filtered through the clouds, caressing the earth with its warm rays, promoting growth and prosperity. It was the breath that drove life, the awakening of each morning that promised new opportunities and hopes.

On the other hand, "The Dark One", rooted in the depths of the world, in a realm where sunlight could not reach, wove the essence of shadow and mystery. His domain was the refuge of the unknown, the sacred space for the unrevealed. From this abode, "The Dark One" sent out currents of dark energy, not as a force of evil, but as the balance necessary for light. It was the darkness that allowed the stars to shine brightly, the restful rest that followed the day, the promise of renewal in the endless cycle of life.

Together, "The Glorious One" and "The Dark One" exercised constant surveillance over the world. Their union symbolized the understanding that neither light without shadow, nor clarity without mystery, could exist in harmony. They were the guarantors that each element, each force of nature, found its place and its purpose in the great design of the cosmos.

If ever a kingdom leaned too far toward one extreme, if the fire threatened to consume everything or if the waters sought to claim more than their due, they intervened. "The Glorious One" could dim rampaging flames with a breeze of light, or "The Dark One" could summon darkness to calm raging storms. Together, they restored order, reminding their dragon brothers and mortals alike of the importance of living in balance.

Throughout the ages, as the nations of the Six Dragons flourished and faced their own challenges, the presence of "The Glorious One" and "The Dark One" remained constant, though increasingly veiled. They became legendary figures, whose interventions were recounted in stories and myths, reminders of a time when gods walked directly among mortals.

Today, although dragons no longer manifest themselves openly in the world, their influence endures. "The Glorious one" and "The Dark One" continue to play their part from the shadows and the light, ensuring that the balance they once established remains the cornerstone upon which the future is built. In every sunrise and sunset, in the duality of existence, his legacy lives on, an eternal reminder that harmony is found in the balance of opposites.

The establishment of the kingdoms under the tutelage of the Six Dragons marked the beginning of an unprecedented era in the history of the world. Each dragon, sovereign of its domain, imprinted its essence and wisdom on the lands and peoples it ruled. However, far from isolating themselves in their respective territories, they established a system of cooperation and trade among themselves, weaving a network of interdependence that strengthened the very fabric of civilization.

The Kingdom of Still Waters, ruled by "The Pacific", provided fish and pearls, and its sailors and merchants sailed the seas, connecting continents and cultures. The Lands of Fire, under the aegis of "The Wild One", shared their advances in metallurgy and crafts that required the intense heat of their forges. The products of these kingdoms were coveted in the markets of other nations, where they were exchanged for equally valuable goods.

On the grasslands ruled by "The Changeling", the nomadic people moved with the seasons, their caravans carrying spices, cloth, and news from one end of the world to the other. Their adaptability and knowledge of trade routes made them essential intermediaries in the trade network that linked the kingdoms.

The Fortresses of the Earth, guarded by "The Firm One", were the origin of precious minerals and gems, as well as grains and vegetables that grew in their fertile valleys. The solidity and stability of this kingdom made it a fundamental pillar in the livelihood and global economy.

Over them all, "The Glorious One" from his City of Light, and "The Dark One" from his Haven of Shadows, kept watch, ensuring that trade and interactions were not only prosperous, but also maintained the essential balance. for life in the world. Their presence, although less visible, was a constant reminder of the need for harmony between light and darkness, creation and preservation.

This network of cooperation and mutual respect between the kingdoms ensured that, while each rejoiced in their uniqueness, they all understood their interconnectedness and the importance of their contribution to the common well-being. Festivals and celebrations often brought together representatives from all kingdoms, where they shared their cultures, knowledge and friendships, strengthening the ties that united them.

The peace that reigned in this golden age was the fruit of the combined wisdom and power of the Six Dragons, whose teachings and legacy permeated every aspect of life. In their kingdoms, war and conflict were distant memories, replaced by a shared commitment to progress and prosperity, always in balance with the natural forces that shaped the world.

Thus, the Six Dragons, more than rulers, became the guardians of an era of enlightenment and harmony. Even as ages change and dragons pass into the realm of legend, the ideal of balance, cooperation and peace they established remains a beacon for all future generations, a testament to what is possible when beings unite for good. common.

Chapter III: The Serenity of Fen in the Pacific Kingdom

In the calm blue waters of the Pacific Kingdom, Fen's life flowed as harmoniously as the tides. Known among his people for his unrivaled skill with net and hook, Fen had built a life of contentment and joy along the shores he loved. Their home, a cozy haven on the shore, overlooked the vast ocean, the source of their livelihood and countless stories told under the glow of the stars.

Life in the Pacific Kingdom was a song of abundance and serenity. The waters, generous and full of life, offered more than enough for all its inhabitants. The teachings of "The Pacific" about sustainability and respect for the sea had penetrated deeply into the heart of Fen, who practiced fishing not only as a way of life, but as a form of communion with nature.

Fen shared this peace and prosperity with his beloved wife, a woman of gentle spirit and easy laughter, who spun webs as skillfully as she told stories to her newborn son. Their son, a spark of joy in their lives, was the link that completed their small world, a promise of continuity and hope.

Every day, at dawn, Fen set out in his boat, gliding over the mirror of the water toward the fishing spots he knew better than himself. And every day, when he returned, his boat was full, not only of fish but of stories and dreams captured among the waves. He was a simple man, yes, but in his simplicity lay profound wisdom: the understanding that true happiness is found in harmony with the world around us and in the love shared with those we call family.

The community that surrounded Fen was a tight knit of souls who shared an unbreakable love for the sea and the ties that bound them together. Parties and gatherings were not uncommon, and in them, music, dancing, and sharing the day's catch reinforced unity and gratitude for the blessings of the ocean.

However, despite the apparent tranquility, the sea holds secrets and mysteries in its depths, and life, even in the Pacific Kingdom, is not without changes and challenges. Fen, although he didn't know it yet, was destined to face trials that would test his spirit and his love for his home and family.

For now, the sun was setting, dyeing the sky in shades of gold and purple, a reflection of the peace that reigned in the kingdom. Fen, with his wife and son at his side, looked toward the horizon, grateful for the blessings of the day and oblivious to the shadows that the near future was beginning to weave over his destiny.

Fen's life in the Pacific kingdom was a melody composed of the whisper of the wind and the constant murmur of the waves. Each day, before the veil of night was withdrawn at the first glimpse of dawn, Fen embarked on his small but sturdy boat, greeting the new day with the hope and vigor that characterized his spirit. Fishing was not only their livelihood; It was the rhythm of his life, an eternal dance with the sea that had seen him grow.

Fen's workday began with the careful selection of nets, woven by his wife's skillful hands, which became extensions of his own arms when he threw them into the sea. He observed the water with expert eyes, reading its secrets as if they were ancient manuscripts, understanding the language of the currents and the song of the fish.

Upon returning home, his heart was filled with a warmth that only family love could offer. His wife's smile and his son's laughter were the treasures he treasured above any material wealth. The afternoons faded into games and laughter, into lessons about the sea and its mysteries, into stories of fishermen and dragons that protected the waters. Dinner, a modest but loving feast, brought the family together in a circle of gratitude and unity.

This cycle of life, marked by simplicity and the satisfaction of essential needs, was Fen's world. He did not long for riches or fame; his wealth was his family, and his fame the stories of his skill and kindness that circulated among his neighbors. His home was his kingdom, and the sea was his eternal friend and provider.

However, one day, returning from a particularly successful day, with the sun bathing the sea in gold and his boat loaded with promises of abundance, Fen felt a change in the air. An imperceptible shadow crossed his heart, an omen that the brightness of the evening could not dispel. With each paddle that brought him closer to shore, a restlessness grew within him, a nameless fear that darkened the light of his spirit.

As she approached her home, the place that had always been her sanctuary of peace and love, Fen couldn't shake the feeling that something had changed. The joyful anticipation that normally drove him to quicken his pace was replaced by a heaviness, a premonition that life as he knew it was about to take an unexpected turn.

The chapter of his existence, until now full of comforting routines and simple joys, was about to close, leaving room for a new page marked by uncertainty. Something terrible had happened, an event that would challenge the strength of his soul and push him on a journey beyond the calm waters of his beloved kingdom.

The day had begun under the auspices of good fortune for Fen, whose nets were filled with the bounty of the sea, heralding a triumphant return home. The sun, as it descended toward the horizon, painted the sky in shades of gold and crimson, a splendid backdrop for the end of a placid day. The sea breeze, impregnated with the salt of the ocean, caressed his face, carrying with it the sweet aroma of the approaching home. With his heart overflowing with joy, Fen could already imagine the warm reception that awaited him, the image of his wife and son shining in his mind like a beacon of love and hope.

However, this idyllic return was abruptly interrupted by an omen of disaster. From the sky, which moments before had appeared as a calm bluish expanse, an imminent threat emerged: a meteor, enveloped in furious flames and dragging with it a trail of black smoke, was hurtling towards the earth with an unstoppable destructive force. The beauty of the sunset was overshadowed by the shadow of the cataclysm, transforming the serenity of the day into a scene of apocalypse.

The impact of the meteor against Fen's home was an event of catastrophic magnitude. The earth trembled under the power of the collision, as if the world itself cried at such an act of violence. The fire from the sky, released by the fiery meteor, was unleashed in a ravenous frenzy, consuming everything in its path. In a matter of seconds, the familiar landscape surrounding Fen's abode was transformed into an inferno, a field of smoldering ruins where once stood a refuge full of life and laughter.

The air was filled with the roar of fire and the crunch of broken earth, a cacophony of destruction that drowned out all hope. The flames, hungry and merciless, danced in a macabre spectacle, devouring memories and dreams with equal voracity. The devastation was absolute, a silent testimony to the relentless power of nature unleashed.

Fen, faced with this scene of desolation, felt hope fading in the ash-laden air. The race toward home, driven by a desperate desire to deny the undeniable, became a slow crawl across an unrecognizable landscape. Each step brought him closer to the reality of his worst nightmare, a world where the light of his life had been extinguished by the fury of the sky.

In this moment of catastrophe, Fen's heart was caught in the storm of emotions that the cataclysm unleashed. The magnitude of the disaster that had befallen him was an abyss that threatened to engulf him, leaving him adrift in a sea of pain and despair. The meteor tragedy was not just a devastating personal loss; It was a cruel reminder of the fragility of existence in the face of the indomitable forces of the universe.

Although the consequences of the disaster remain veiled, the resilience of the human spirit shines even in the darkest moments, propelling Fen forward on his path to redemption and rebirth.

In the darkest moment of his life, Fen found himself standing among the charred remains of what was once his home, his sanctuary of love and joy. The meteor's devastating impact had left an indelible scar not only on the land, but on Fen's very soul. What had been a hopeful return became a living nightmare, an abyss of despair that engulfed him with its implacable darkness.

The bodies of his wife and son lay before him, silent witnesses to the tragedy that had torn his world apart. The pain that washed over Fen was so deep, so overwhelming, that words couldn't begin to describe it. It was as if every beat of his heart resonated with a cry of anguish, a symphony of desolation that drowned out any hint of light within him.

Fen's tears mixed with the gently falling rain, as if the sky itself shared her grief, crying over the injustice of such a great loss. Every drop that touched his skin was a reminder of the love and warmth that had now been extinguished, leaving him alone in the immensity of his suffering.

He looked up at the meteor, that mass of destruction that had fallen from the sky like an omen of death. Anger and despair were intertwined in his gaze, a storm of emotions desperately searching for who to blame, how to make sense of such a blind act of cruelty. But there were no answers in the flames that still licked at the remains of his past, only the emptiness that devoured his hope.

The peace that had characterized Fen's existence, the serenity of the Pacific kingdom that had been his home, vanished in an instant. Tragedy had struck with such force that the future, once full of promise and dreams, now seemed a distant, unattainable horizon, obscured by clouds of despair.

In his grief, Fen felt torn from reality, floating in a limbo of sadness and rage. The realization that his life would never be the same hit him with the force of a storm, leaving him teetering on the edge of an abyss of despair. The question of "Why?" It resonated in his mind, an endless echo that searched for answers in a universe that had suddenly become hostile and meaningless.

Thus, with a broken heart and a soul plunged into darkness, Fen faced the greatest challenge of his existence. The tragedy had marked the end of a chapter of his life, but also the beginning of a path that would take him along unknown paths, in search of justice, redemption and perhaps, one day, the peace that had existed.

With the weight of grief anchored in his spirit, Fen made the most difficult resolution of his life: to leave behind the ruins of his past existence and enter the unknown, driven by the need to understand and, if possible, find justice for the man. immense emptiness that now consumed him. Armed only with his determination and pain as a constant companion, he began a journey that would take him beyond the confines of his knowledge and his world.

Fen's path was fraught with uncertainty and danger. Each step away from the calm waters of his home submerged him deeper into a strange territory, where the shadows of tragedy seemed to lengthen with each sunset. The destruction caused by the meteor had left a visible scar on the land, a trail of desolation that Fen followed with a mixture of fear and determination.

On her journey, Fen faced challenges she never could have imagined. Creatures of the night and bandits lurked on the roads less traveled, and more than once, his life hung by a thread, saved only by his wits and iron will. However, these dangers pale in comparison to the internal battle he waged, fighting the hopelessness and anger that threatened to consume him.

Despite the adversities, Fen did not allow his spirit to be broken. In each village or city he visited, he searched for answers, collecting stories and legends that could shed light on the meteor's origin and its purpose. But the answers were elusive, hidden in layers of myth and speculation that did little to quench his thirst for truth.

Fen's journey became an odyssey, a pilgrimage marked by pain but driven by the faint hope that one day she might understand the reason behind the tragedy that had torn her life apart. With each new dawn, he reminded himself why he must continue, why he could not afford to give in to the abyss of despair.

Although the road offered few answers and each night brought with it the same searing pain from the loss of her family, Fen found a strange strength in her search. It was the spark of determination, a fire that, although threatened by the storms of doubt, refused to go out.

Thus, Fen's journey became more than a search for justice; It became the path of a man who, through suffering and challenge, sought to find his place in a world he no longer recognized. Unknown to him, Fen was being forged by his trials, prepared for a destiny that was intertwined with the deepest mysteries of the world and the legacy of the Six Dragons. For now, however, the answers remained as elusive as the shadows at nightfall, and the road ahead stretched, filled with uncertainties and promises of revelations yet to be discovered.

As Fen progressed on his odyssey, the fabric of stories and legends he collected became a complex tapestry, full of threads that weaved the story of a world far more vast and enigmatic than he had ever imagined. The villages he passed through, the elders he spoke with, and the dusty books he managed to find in markets and forgotten libraries revealed fragments of a past marked by titanic conflicts and incomprehensible powers.

One of the most recurring narratives that resonated most in Fen's heart was that of the ancient war between the Six Dragons, beings of unimaginable power whose disputes had once shaken the foundations of the world. I listened, with growing amazement, as these dragons, living representations of the elements, had fought battles that shaped mountains, diverted rivers, and reconfigured the landscape of the world.

But what most captured Fen's attention and ignited a spark of fear in his heart was the discovery that, even in this era of peace, there were those who longed for the return of those tumultuous days. According to legends, hidden sects and forgotten cults sought to revive the power and fury of dragons, once again unleashing primordial forces in a bid for power and dominance.

These revelations filled Fen with deep concern. The idea that there were those who wished to disturb the harmony of the world, sowing chaos and imbalance for dark ambitions, was something he could not understand. How could anyone long for the return of an era marked by destruction and suffering?

Throughout his travels, Fen encountered ancient ruins and stone markers that told stories of forgotten battles, of alliances and betrayals among the dragons, and how they had finally found a path to peace. Every stone, every fragment of story, was a reminder of how much was at stake if the forces seeking to destabilize the world achieved their goal.

Fen's resolve was strengthened by these discoveries. He now understood that his quest was not just personal, but was intrinsically connected to the fate of the entire world. The tragedy that had devastated his life was possibly just a piece in a much larger game, a warning of what could be unleashed if the balance between the kingdoms was broken.

With each new clue he followed, each legend he discovered, Fen delved deeper into the labyrinth of ancient history, seeking not only answers to his own loss, but also a way to confront the shadows that loomed on the horizon. Their journey, begun by the deepest pain, had transformed into a quest of epic proportions, in which the echo of Fen's footsteps resonated not only through the realms of the dragons, but through time itself, in an attempt to preserve light in a world that threatened to be consumed by darkness once again.

As Fen continued on his quest, every discovery, every fragment of truth he unearthed from the shadows of the past, fueled the fire of revenge in his heart. The determination that had driven him to leave behind the ruins of his old life was now transformed into unbreakable resolve. It wasn't just the desire for answers that moved him; It was the need for justice, a silent promise to the loved ones he had lost that their suffering would not go unanswered.

This internal fire became the compass that guided each of his steps, a flame that illuminated his path even in the darkest moments. Fen, who had once been a simple fisherman whose life revolved around the tides and the fishing seasons, now found himself at the center of a plot that spanned the very foundations of the world. And although the magnitude of his mission sometimes overwhelmed him, his determination never wavered.

With each city he visited, each scholar he conversed with, and each ancient text he studied, Fen pieced together the vast puzzle that was the history of dragons and the forces that sought to once again unleash chaos on the world. He learned of the delicate balances that kept kingdoms in harmony, of ancient pacts that had been forged in a time where war between powerful beings threatened to tear the fabric of reality.

But more importantly, Fen began to understand the nature of his enemy. These were not just isolated individuals or dark cults operating in the shadows; It was a current of thought, a thirst for power and domination that had infected hearts through the centuries. The tragedy that had destroyed his family was, perhaps, just a symptom of a much deeper illness.

This realization filled him with a mixture of fear and anger, but also with a strange hope. If he had learned anything on his journey, it was that the brightest light is often found in the darkest depths. The same determination that had driven him to seek revenge now drove him to go further, to find a solution that would not only end his own suffering, but also protect the world from future tragedies.

Fen swore to himself and the memory of his wife and son that he would not rest until those responsible for his pain were brought to justice, and that he would do everything in his power to prevent other families from suffering as he had suffered. . This oath, born of love and loss, became his guiding light, a light in the darkness that reminded him that even in the midst of the most heartbreaking pain, one has the power to make a difference.

Thus, with each step forward, Fen came closer to the truth, armed with the knowledge of the ancients and a will of steel. Their journey was proof that even the humblest of mortals could face the deepest shadows, defying the forces that sought to plunge the world into despair. And in his heart, the certainty that, in the end, the light would find a way.

As Fen moved forward in his tireless search for answers and justice, his story began to echo like an echo across the Pacific realm, spreading from village to village, island to island. What had begun as the lonely journey of a wounded man transformed into a tale of courage and resilience that touched the hearts of those who heard it.

The fishermen who cast their nets under the same vast sky under which Fen had sailed told their story during the long nights at sea. Families who gathered around the fire on the beaches shared his legend, seeing in Fen not just a fisherman, but a hero who had risen from tragedy to face the shadows that threatened his world.

His determination to uncover the truth and demand justice for his lost family became a beacon of hope for many. In a time where tranquility and happiness seemed guaranteed, Fen's story reminded everyone of the fragility of peace and the importance of fighting to maintain it. His name became synonymous with fighting adversity, a symbol that even in the darkest moments, one can rise up and face challenges.

As his fame grew, so did the number of those who wished to aid him in his mission. Some offered him shelter and food; others, knowledge and advice. With each new ally, Fen realized that his personal journey had become something much greater: a crusade for justice and balance that united people from all corners of the kingdom.

Fen had become an iconic figure, the embodiment of resistance against the forces that sought to destabilize the order established by the Six Dragons. His story inspired others to look beyond their daily lives, to recognize that they were part of a larger fabric, interconnected by threads of destiny and shared responsibility.

The path Fen was traveling was, without a doubt, dangerous and full of uncertainties. Every day brought new challenges, every revelation, more questions. However, his unwavering will to move forward, to fight for what was right, had become a rallying cry for those who believed in a world where the light of justice could triumph over the darkness of chaos and destruction.

At the confluence of his destiny with that of the Six Dragons and their ancient kingdoms, Fen was not alone. He was accompanied by the hope and support of an entire people who saw in him the possibility of preserving the harmony and peace that they had valued so much. Although the end of her journey was still shrouded in mystery, Fen's determination and courage lit the way, a beacon of hope in the fight to restore balance to a world on the brink of change.

Chapter IV: Revelation at the Summit

Fen's quest took him through countless dangers and challenges, each overcome with the steely determination of one who has little to lose and everything to gain. His journey, which had begun in the calm waters of his home, now found him in the remotest reaches of the Pacific kingdom, where the waves whispered forgotten secrets and the sea breezes carried echoes of ancient truths.

It was in this place, guided by the chief of a town who seemed to know the mysteries of the world better than anyone, where Fen found the key to unraveling the enigma of his tragedy. With the wisdom shared by this ancient leader, whose knowledge seemed to transcend time, Fen ventured to the summit of a mountain that stood like a silent guardian on the outskirts of the kingdom.

The climb was arduous, a physical reflection of the internal struggle Fen had been waging since the day of the catastrophe. With each step toward the top, I felt the truth draw closer, tangible but still veiled in shadows. It was there, at the top of the mountain, that Fen discovered the unimaginable.

Remnants of ancient rituals and arcane magic littered the site, evidence of a conspiracy that had upset the natural balance to call upon the meteor's destructive fury. And among the rubble of ancient stone and ash, Fen found confirmation of his worst fears: the attack that had devastated his life was not a whim of fate, but a deliberate act, a disastrous alliance between the realms of fire and earth.

The revelation filled Fen with uncontrollable fury, a storm of rage that threatened to consume him from within. The betrayal of those who should have been guardians of balance, who in their excessive ambition had unleashed a force capable of annihilating innocent lives, ignited in Fen a desire for revenge that surpassed any fear.

With a heavy heart but an unbreakable will, Fen realized that his search had reached a turning point. The truth behind the tragedy he had suffered now propelled him toward a new goal: confront those responsible and demand justice for the acts that had torn his world apart.

Armed with the knowledge of the conspiracy and a determination forged in the fire of loss, Fen descended the mountain, no longer the fisherman he once was, but as a warrior willing to fight for justice. His journey, far from ending, had taken a new direction, one that would lead him to confront the forces that sought to unbalance the world.

Fen's resolve was clear: he would find those who had orchestrated the meteor fall and bring them to justice, no matter the cost. In his heart, a promise burned brighter than ever: he would not allow any more families to suffer the same fate as his own. With truth as his banner and justice as his guide, Fen prepared for the battle ahead, determined to restore the balance that had been broken.

The revelation about the alliance between the kingdoms of fire and earth had left Fen with a deep feeling of despair, faced with enemies whose power surpassed everything imaginable. However, determination and love for his family and his kingdom drove him to seek a solution, leading him to an almost forgotten legend: the Water Dragon, the guardian of the depths and lord of the seas and rivers.

Hoping to gain the power needed to restore balance, Fen entered the heart of the water kingdom, a domain where the waters danced to an ancient melody and where the Water Dragon was said to reside. The journey was not easy; The waters he had known all his life now seemed full of mysteries and challenges. Every wave, every current seemed to test his resolve, as if the sea itself were evaluating the dignity and worth of his cause.

Guided by ancient stars and the whispers of the wind, Fen sailed through storms and calm seas, always with the vision of his goal clear in his mind. Stories of fishermen and time-worn maps guided him to where the waters grew darker and the deepest secrets were hidden in the gloom of the abyss.

After days of tireless searching, as the sun sank below the horizon and painted the sky in hues of fire and blood, Fen arrived at what seemed to be the end of the known world. There, where the waters sank into the depths and the horizon was lost in the mist, he found the entrance to the palace of the Water Dragon.

It was a place of unfathomable beauty, where columns of coral rose like towers toward the surface and schools of luminous fish weaved patterns of light in the darkness. The palace, built in the depths where no mortal had dared to venture, revealed itself to Fen as a promise of hope and power. With its ethereal structure, it seemed both a part of the sea and a monument to the majesty of the Water Dragon.

At the threshold of this underwater kingdom, Fen felt a mixture of awe and fear. He had reached the heart of the Water Dragon's domain, the place where his search would find its answer. The magnitude of what he was about to do, asking for help from a being whose existence was intertwined with the foundations of the world, filled him with profound humility.

Armed only with his determination and the justice of his cause, Fen prepared to enter the palace and face the Water Dragon. He didn't know what awaited him in the shadows of that sacred place, but he was ready to face it, for his family, his kingdom, and the balance of the world. At that moment, on the threshold between the known and the unknown, Fen's story took a new turn, leading him toward an encounter that would define the course of his destiny.

Upon entering the submerged realm, Fen found that the path to the Water Dragon, "The Pacific", was guarded by trials that tested not only his courage and skill, but also the purity of his heart and sincerity. of your search. Each challenge seemed designed to interrogate his resolve, to unravel the very essence of his being.

The first test confronted him with tumultuous currents that sought to drag him away from the palace. With determination, Fen swam through them, using his knowledge of the sea to find the correct path, demonstrating his respect and understanding of the waters that "The Pacific" governed.

Fen then found himself in a vast room where mirages of his worst fears materialized before him. Visions of his destroyed home and lost loved ones haunted him, trying to break his spirit. However, Fen, fueled by the memory of his family and the need for justice, broke through the illusion, showing his inner strength and his ability to face and overcome his pain.

The third and final test was a labyrinth of brilliant corals, an enigma that challenged their intelligence and patience. This labyrinth, full of beauty and danger, symbolized the intricate paths of destiny. Fen, guided by the light of his conviction, found his way out, demonstrating his willingness to seek the truth, no matter how convoluted the path.

By overcoming these tests, Fen reached the heart of the palace, where the water calmed and time seemed to stop. There, in the center of a room illuminated by light filtered through the water, lay "The Pacific", in a torpor that seemed to have lasted for eons. The dragon's presence was overwhelming, a reminder of the power that ruled the seas and oceans.

With humility and hope, Fen told his story, telling of the attack that had destroyed everything he loved, fueled by the alliance between the kingdom of fire and earth. His voice, charged with emotion, resonated in the silence of the room, seeking to awaken compassion in the dragon's heart.

"The Pacific" opened its eyes, like two oceanic abysses that reflected the immensity of the sea. He listened carefully, his expression an enigma. The wisdom of millennia was glimpsed in his gaze, understanding Fen's pain and determination. However, his response remained in suspense, leaving Fen in a sea of uncertainty.

Fen's story had reached the ears of the guardian of the waters, but the Water Dragon's verdict, and the fate of Fen's quest, were yet to be determined. In that sacred moment, with the future hanging in the balance, Fen waited, his heart beating to the rhythm of the waves, knowing that what "The Pacific" decided would change the course of his life and, possibly, that of the entire world.

In the depths of the underwater palace, facing the imposing presence of the Water Dragon, "The Pacific", Fen found himself at a crucial moment in his journey. The revelation of the conspiracy between the kingdoms of fire and earth had led him to seek the power necessary to confront such enemies, a power that only an ancient and powerful entity like "The Pacific" could provide. However, the dragon's help was not something to be granted lightly.

"The Pacific", with his voice evoking the calm roar of distant waves, expressed concern about the implications of granting such power to a mortal. "Fen, your heart is pure and your cause is just, but you must understand that the power you seek has the potential to upset the balance of the world. The actions you take with it may have consequences far beyond your quest for justice. "Are you prepared to assume this responsibility and face the possible repercussions of your actions?"

The gravity of the situation weighed on Fen, whose feelings of determination were now mixed with deep reflection on the consequences of his actions. The decision to accept the power offered by "The Pacific" was not just a matter of personal revenge, but one that could affect the delicate fabric of existence itself. In his heart, Fen knew that the path to justice was full of challenges and sacrifices, but he also understood that fighting for the greater good required courage and an unwavering will to do what was right, despite the risks.

With resolve strengthened by the realization of the implications of his choice, Fen responded with a conviction that echoed in the silence of the palace. "I am fully aware of the responsibilities that this power entails. I accept the consequences of my actions, for my desire is not only to avenge those I lost, but to prevent such tragedies from being repeated. For them, for my kingdom, and for the balance of the world, I am willing to carry this weight."

The Water Dragon looked at Fen, analyzing the sincerity and firmness in his words. There was a mix of respect and sadness in the dragon's eyes, aware of the burden he was about to place on Fen's shoulders. However, there was also hope, a belief that this mortal could be the key to preserving the balance he himself had sworn to protect.

The decision was made. "The Pacific" recognized in Fen someone worthy of his trust and support, a warrior whose fight transcended personal desire and touched the very heart of the world's destiny. However, the ritual that would seal their pact and grant Fen the power he sought had yet to take place, a moment of transformation that would define both of their futures.

Thus, with a mutual understanding of the consequences that their actions could trigger, Fen and "The Pacific" prepared to take the next step in this unprecedented alliance. The path Fen had chosen was full of uncertainties, but with the support of the Water Dragon, he would face the challenges that awaited him, armed with new strength and the determination to change the course of destiny.

With the power of water newly granted by "The Pacific", Fen felt a surge of determination and purpose revitalize his spirit. This new power not only strengthened him physically, but also strengthened his resolve to confront the injustices that had devastated his life and threatened to unbalance the world. The journey ahead, full of uncertainties and dangers, no longer seemed so insurmountable. Now, more than ever, he was ready to wage the battle necessary to restore harmony.

Preparation for their next trip was meticulous and deliberate. Fen knew that facing the realms of fire and earth would require not only strength, but also strategy and wisdom. He gathered supplies, studied old maps, and learned about the lands he would have to traverse. Each step was calculated to maximize his chances of success in the mission he had set for himself.

Furthermore, Fen spent time becoming familiar with the power that now coursed through his veins. He practiced controlling the force of water, learning to manipulate it for defense and attack. He discovered that he could call the waters to his will, creating eddies and waves with a simple gesture of his hand. This mastery over the element gave him a significant tactical advantage, a powerful tool against enemies who dared to challenge him.

As the days passed, the time for departure approached. Fen stood on the shore of the Pacific kingdom, looking towards the horizon where the sun was beginning to set, coloring the sky in fiery tones. The irony of heading towards the kingdom of fire under such a spectacle was not lost on him. It was as if the skies themselves marked the path to their destination.

Fen's destiny, irrevocably intertwined with that of the Six Dragons and the kingdoms they once ruled in harmony, was about to take a new turn. Armed with the power of water and unwavering determination, he was ready to face the challenges that awaited him in the lands of fire. The coming war would not just be a battle for personal revenge, but an effort to preserve the balance of the world and protect the innocent from the destructive ambitions of a few.

As night fell and the stars began to shine in the sky, Fen took one last look at the calm waters that had been his home. Then, with a sigh of resolution, he turned and started toward his destination. The image of Fen, silhouetted against the twilight, marked the beginning of a day that could change the destiny of the world. With the firm heart and indomitable spirit that had always characterized him, he stepped into the darkness, ready to face whatever was necessary in the name of justice and harmony.

Chapter V: The Prelude to the Fire Tournament

As Fen set out on his path toward an uncertain destiny, armed with the new strength conferred by "The Pacific", an event of legendary magnitude was brewing in the distant kingdom of fire. The Fire Tournament, a tradition rooted in the history and culture of the kingdom, was approaching, enveloping the kingdom in a blanket of anticipation and fervor. This event, held every four years, was not just a competition; It was a rite of passage, a link between the past and the future, between mortals and the divine.

The flames that illuminated the fiery coliseum were a spectacle in themselves, dancing in harmony with the emotions and expectations of the thousands of spectators who gathered to witness the tournament. The hot air vibrated with the energy of the promises and dreams of the competitors, each one longing to become the next champion, the chosen one who would have the honor of communicating with "The Wild One", the Dragon of Fire.

The privilege of receiving a part of the dragon's power made the tournament a matter of great importance, not only for the competitors but for the entire kingdom. This gift was seen as a blessing, a strengthening of the bond that united the kingdom of fire with its ancestral protector. It was a palpable demonstration of the dragon's presence and favor, a force that propelled the kingdom forward, protecting it and guiding it through the ages.

The night before the tournament began, the kingdom was in a state of ferment. The streets echoed with the clamor of preparations, the voices of the citizens mixing with the crackling of the flames. Artisans and merchants displayed their best works and products, from armor and weapons forged with the purest fire to foods and drinks that promised to strengthen the body and spirit of competitors.

In the squares and taverns, stories of tournaments past were shared with reverence, each tale a reminder of the honor and glory that awaited the champion. The oldest in the crowd spoke of legendary champions, whose names and deeds had been immortalized in the history of the kingdom. For young people, these stories were a source of inspiration, a call to overcome their own limits and forge their legend.

As the moon rose in the night sky, bathing the kingdom in its silvery light, the fiery coliseum stood majestically, its imposing silhouette a constant reminder of what was at stake. Inside, echoing flames and dancing shadows created a sanctuary for the spirit of fire, setting the stage for the drama that would unfold under its watch.

The Fire Tournament was more than a competition; It was a moment of unity for the kingdom, a celebration of its strength, its passion, and its eternal connection to "The Wild One". As dawn approached, marking the start of the tournament, the kingdom of fire waited with bated breath, knowing that the events that would unfold in the coliseum would define the future of the kingdom and, perhaps, the entire world.

As dawn colored the sky in shades of fire and gold, announcing the start of the Fire Tournament, the coliseum became the meeting point for the bravest and most skilled warriors of the kingdom and beyond. The excitement was palpable in the air, heavy with the scent of smoke and the promise of epic battles. This year, the expectation was even greater, fueled by rumors of a competitor whose humble origins contrasted with the immense potential he seemed to hide.

Kaen, a warrior with an almost ethereal presence, came from a small town on the edge of the kingdom, where the flames danced freely and the heat of the sun never diminished. Until now, his name had been just one among many seeking glory and honor in the tournament. However, as the time of the competition approached, stories of his skill and unwavering determination began to circulate with fervor among those in attendance.

The other warriors, some veterans of previous tournaments and others thirsty for recognition, watched Kaen with a mixture of curiosity and wariness. Despite his modest origins, there was something about his bearing and the way he handled his weapon—a sword that seemed forged in the very bowels of a volcano—that spoke of a strength and skill that could not be underestimated.

As the competitors arrived at the coliseum, the atmosphere was filled with intense energy. Armor gleamed in the morning sun, and the sound of steel clashing during final adjustments echoed like a prelude to the battles to come. Each warrior carried the hope of his people, the ambition of his heart, and the weight of the tradition that this tournament represented.

Among them, Kaen moved with a serenity that contrasted with the frenzy around him. His eyes, fixed on the horizon of the coliseum, reflected not only the determination to achieve victory, but also a deep respect for the challenge he was about to face. He was not just looking for the title of champion; For him, this tournament was a test of his own worth, a path toward a destiny he felt compelled to discover.

Kaen's arrival at the coliseum not only marked the beginning of his own journey to glory, but it also signaled a change in the air, a feeling that this tournament would reveal something unexpected and extraordinary. As the competitors took their places and the public filled the stands, the figure of Kaen, now the center of attention, stood as the promise of a tournament that would be remembered for generations.

Kaen's destiny was yet to be written, and the fire coliseum, with its history of honor and sacrifice, would be the setting where his legend would begin to take shape. In this crucible of fire and ambition, Kaen prepared to prove that even the most unknown warrior could rise and claim his place among the stars.

The beginning of the Fire Tournament was marked by the traditional demonstration of skills, where each competitor had the opportunity to impress the public and their opponents with a display of their strength, skill and mastery of the element that gave its name to the kingdom. The warriors displayed an array of impressive techniques, from the masterful handling of weapons engulfed in flames to the execution of gravity-defying maneuvers, each seeking to secure their place in the memory of the spectators.

Amid these impressive displays, Kaen remained enigmatic, his participation in the preliminary exhibition subtle, almost discreet. He performed basic movements, showing respectable competence but without revealing the fullness of his ability. In the eyes of the spectators, he seemed to be just another competitor in the sea of talents seeking glory in the coliseum. However, this perception was about to change dramatically.

When the time came for their first real fight, the atmosphere in the coliseum was charged with anticipation. His opponent, a warrior renowned for his aggression and ability to manipulate fire in destructive ways, underestimated Kaen, considering him less of a challenge. This underestimation would prove to be his downfall.

From the moment the start signal sounded, Kaen was transformed. His previously reserved movements became quick and precise, a dance of agility and power that left his opponent and the spectators in awe. With every dodge, every attack, Kaen demonstrated a mastery of combat that went beyond mere physical skill; It was as if he were in harmony with the same fire that sought to dominate him.

The combat was brief but intense. Kaen not only evaded each of his opponent's fierce attacks, but also countered them with a series of moves that culminated in a decisive blow. The defeat of his opponent was not only physical; It was a clear message to everyone present that Kaen was a competitor whose true potential was yet to be fully revealed.

The audience was silent for a moment, processing what they had just witnessed. Then the coliseum erupted in applause, murmurs of amazement and admiration woven into a chorus of speculation and respect. Who was this warrior who, out of nowhere, had proven to be a master of combat? How had he acquired such skill, and what else could he be hiding?

Kaen, for his part, accepted the victory with a serenity that contrasted with the intensity of his performance. Although he had revealed some of his skill, he knew that the road to the title of champion was still long and that each fight would test not only his strength but also his spirit.

Thus, with a single combat, Kaen went from being a mysterious rookie to becoming the center of all eyes, his name whispered with a mixture of admiration and curiosity. The tournament still had many battles ahead, but it was already clear that Kaen would be an undisputed protagonist in the history that would be written in the fire of that coliseum.

With each battle he faced, Kaen not only overcame obstacles, but also wove his own legend in the heart of the kingdom of fire. His skill and prowess in the art of combat seemed supernatural, defying the expectations of spectators and raising the level of tournament competition to unprecedented heights. His presence in the arena, serene but imposing, captured everyone's attention, creating an aura of expectation every time he prepared to fight.

Competitors facing Kaen found it a challenge like no other. Every movement he made was loaded with a precision and efficiency that left little room for response. Its attacks, fluid like the course of a river of lava, always found its mark, while its defenses were impassable, like the walls of the most fortified citadel. As Kaen progressed through the tournament, defeating each opponent with a grace that bordered on artistic, his fame grew exponentially.

The public, fascinated by this enigmatic warrior, began to weave stories and speculations about his origin. The idea that Kaen could be a dragon in disguise, participating in the tournament to test the limits of mortals or to search for a worthy champion, was not a far-fetched theory to them. After all, how else to explain the magnitude of his power and ability?

Legends about Kaen began to circulate throughout the kingdom, each tale adding another layer to his mysterious figure. Some said he had been secretly trained by "The Wild One" himself, as his chosen champion. Others claimed that it was the reunion of an ancient hero of fire, reborn to lead the kingdom into a new era of glory. Regardless of the truth, Kaen had become a symbol of pride for the fire people, a cause for celebration and admiration.

However, for Kaen, these stories and speculations were foreign to his true purpose. His participation in the tournament was not to seek personal glory or to confirm the legends that were woven around him. His goal was deeper, driven by a search for justice and the need to face a greater challenge that awaited him beyond the coliseum.

As the tournament neared its climax, with only the strongest and most skilled competitors still standing, Kaen prepared for the final tests that would determine his fate and that of the kingdom. With each victory, he was one step closer to facing "The Wild One", to receiving a part of his power, and perhaps, to unraveling the mystery of his own existence.

The legend of Kaen, the warrior whose skill transcended the human, would continue to grow, regardless of the outcome of the tournament. He had already left an indelible mark on the realm of fire, one that would be remembered and told for generations. But for Kaen, there was only one way forward: forward, toward the fulfillment of his destiny, whatever it might be.

As the sun began its descent, coloring the sky with shades of copper and gold, the atmosphere in the coliseum of fire was charged with palpable electricity. It was the eve of the final battle of the Fire Tournament, and all eyes were on two figures: Kaen, the enigmatic challenger whose ascendancy through the tournament had been meteoric, and the reigning champion, whose mastery of fire and experience in combat They had kept him undefeated until now.

In the hours before the confrontation, Kaen sank into a state of deep meditation, searching within himself for the calm and clarity necessary to face the challenge that lay ahead. Around him, the bustle of the coliseum seemed to fade, leaving him alone with his thoughts and the steady pulse of his determination. It wasn't just the championship title that was at stake; For Kaen, this battle was one more step on his path towards a greater purpose, a rehearsal of the fight he knew he must wage in the future.

The reigning champion, for his part, prepared himself with a ritual of strength and fire. Surrounded by flames that danced to the rhythm of his movements, the warrior tempered his spirit and body for combat. Respected for his power and feared for his ferocity, the champion did not underestimate Kaen; he had seen her rise, her ability to outmaneuver every opponent with a mix of grace and relentless strength.

When the moment of the duel finally arrived, the entire coliseum held its breath. The two combatants met in the center of the arena, their silhouettes silhouetted against the glow of the fire that surrounded them. A salute, a mutual recognition of bravery and skill, and the combat began.

It was a battle that seemed to surpass the limits of mortality. Kaen, moving with supernatural speed and precision, met every attack from his adversary with an impenetrable defense, returning blow for blow with a skill that left the audience breathless. The champion, for his part, demonstrated why he had held his title for so long, channeling the power of fire into devastating attacks that lit up the night.

The flames surrounding the coliseum seemed alive, reacting to the intensity of the combat, rising and roaring with each exchange between the two warriors. It was a dance of fire and shadows, a test of will and power where each movement could be the last.

As the fight dragged on, it was evident that Kaen wasn't just there to win; He was there to demonstrate that his presence in the tournament was not the result of chance, but of destiny. With every move, every blow, he wrote his name in the history of the kingdom of fire, defying expectations and surpassing the limits of what was thought possible.

The outcome of the battle remained uncertain, with both combatants fighting with fierce determination. But regardless of the outcome, Kaen had already left his mark, transforming the Fire Tournament into the scene of his revelation, not only as a warrior of immense talent, but as a symbol of change and hope for the kingdom of fire. The conclusion of this epic duel loomed on the horizon, an ending that would be remembered for generations, regardless of who emerged as the victor.

The climax of the final battle of the Fire Tournament loomed, with each blow and movement pushing the two combatants to the limit of their strength. In the charged air of the coliseum, the confrontation between Kaen and the reigning champion had become a living legend, a spectacle of skill, power and determination that would be remembered for centuries.

The tension was broken with a final blow, a move that Kaen had guarded, perfected through each previous fight, a technique that fused not only his physical skill but the deep understanding of fire he had developed throughout the tournament. With overwhelming precision and power, Kaen managed to overcome the defenses of the reigning champion, delivering a blow that sealed the fate of the fight.

The silence that followed was brief, a moment suspended in time where everyone processed the monumental changing of the guard they had just witnessed. Then, as if the coliseum itself awoke from a dream, it burst into deafening applause. Cheers and applause filled the air, celebrating not only Kaen's victory but also the birth of a new legend in the kingdom of fire.

The defeated champion, outmatched but not disgraced, bowed before Kaen, graciously acknowledging his defeat. This show of respect between warriors was a testament to the nobility inherent in the tournament, a tradition that valued honor in defeat as much as in victory.

Kaen, now crowned as the new champion of the Fire Tournament, stood in the center of the coliseum, his figure bathed in the light of the flames that surrounded him. His gaze, fixed on the horizon, reflected not only the satisfaction of victory but also the awareness of the path that still lay ahead. Obtaining the title was just the beginning; He now carried the weight of a much greater responsibility, that of being the protector and leader of the kingdom of fire.

The celebration continued long after the coliseum's flames had dimmed. Throughout the city, the streets were filled with festivities, with music, dance and fireworks lighting up the night. The people of the fire kingdom celebrated not only their new champion but also the promise of a bright future under his leadership.

Kaen, in the midst of the celebration, allowed himself a moment of reflection. Victory in the tournament had granted him the privilege of speaking with "The Wild One" and receiving a portion of his power, an opportunity he had looked forward to with anticipation and respect. He knew that this was only the beginning of his true mission, one that would take him beyond the limits of the coliseum, towards even greater challenges and adventures.

As the night faded into the first light of dawn, Kaen looked toward the future, ready to assume his destiny as the champion of the kingdom of fire, bearer of its legacy, and guardian of its people. The legend of Kaen, the warrior who had risen from the darkness to claim the light, had just begun.

The news of Kaen's victory in the Fire Tournament spread like a wildfire through the kingdom, reaching every village, every city and every corner where the heat of the flames was a constant in daily life. It wasn't just the fact that a new champion had been crowned; It was the way Kaen had risen, defeating each opponent with skill and power that seemed supernatural, that captured the imagination of the people.

Kaen's triumph not only marked the end of a tournament, but also symbolized the beginning of a new era for the kingdom of fire. People began to see in him not only an exceptional warrior, but a potential leader, someone who could guide the kingdom into a future of glory and prosperity. His story, that of an unknown who had risen to claim the most coveted title in the kingdom, resonated with the hope that anyone, no matter their background, could achieve greatness.

In the taverns and public squares, the citizens of the kingdom of fire argued passionately about the tournament and the surprising outcome. While some speculated about Kaen's combat techniques and possible secret training, others immersed themselves in debates about what his victory meant for the future of the kingdom. Rumors about his identity flourished, each one more fantastic than the last. Some claimed that he was a direct descendant of "The Wild One", selected by the dragon himself to carry on his legacy. Others suggested that Kaen was the reincarnation of an ancient fire hero, returned to protect the kingdom in times of need.

As these stories intertwined and grew, Kaen remained enigmatic, his true story shrouded in the mystery of his silence. His reluctance to reveal details about his past only fueled the public's fascination, turning him into an almost mythical figure. However, to those who looked beyond the legends and rumors, it was clear that Kaen possessed a deep connection to fire, one that went beyond skill and training. It was an affinity born of the soul, an unbreakable bond with the element that defined his realm.

In the weeks following his victory, Kaen became the dominant topic of conversation in the kingdom of fire. His image was revered, and his name was pronounced with respect and admiration. Bards began to compose songs in his honor, chronicling his rise from obscurity to champion, and artists portrayed him in their works, capturing the essence of his strength and mystery.

Although the tournament had ended, the legend of Kaen was just beginning to be written. Their victory had lit a spark of hope and pride in the heart of the fire kingdom, a flame that would burn brightly for years to come. Kaen had shown that, even in a world ruled by power and tradition, the courage of an individual could shine with an inextinguishable light, illuminating the path to the future.

After celebrating his victory in the Fire Tournament, Kaen found himself on the threshold of a new stage in his life. With the reverence and expectation of the entire kingdom of fire as witnesses, he headed towards the sacred chambers of "The Wild One", the place where his transformation from champion to sovereign, from mortal to legend, would be consummated.

The walk to meet the Fire Dragon was shrouded in solemn silence, a stark contrast to the joy and celebration that still echoed through the streets of the kingdom. Kaen, wrapped in his thoughts, advanced with a mixture of determination and humility. This moment was the culmination of their incredible journey, the turning point that would define their destiny and, possibly, the future of the entire kingdom.

Arriving at "The Wild One's" chambers, Kaen paused for a moment to collect his thoughts. The place emanated intense heat and primordial energy, as if the very heart of the fire was beating within it. With a deep breath, Kaen crossed the threshold, entering the dragon's domain.

What happened within those sacred chambers would remain a mystery to the rest of the kingdom. Only Kaen and "The Wild One" witnessed the exchange and the ritual that marked the transmission of the dragon's power to the new ruler of fire. It was a moment that transcended words, a pact sealed in the flames of eternity.

When Kaen emerged into the light again, something about him had changed. Although his outward appearance remained unchanged, the intensity of his gaze and the aura of power that surrounded him spoke of a profound transformation. He had entered the chambers as the champion of the Tournament of Fire, but he emerged as the rightful ruler of the kingdom, invested with a fraction of the power and wisdom of "The Wild One."

The entire kingdom waited in suspense, eager to know what words had been shared between the dragon and its new champion. But Kaen, aware of the weight of his new responsibility, remained silent about the details of their meeting. His journey had been long and his battle hard, but he knew this was just the beginning. Now, as ruler and protector of the kingdom of fire, he would face even greater challenges.

News of his coronation and the blessing of "The Wild One" spread quickly through the kingdom, inspiring a mixture of amazement, hope and speculation among its people. Kaen, once a mysterious warrior from nowhere, was now their leader, a beacon of strength and guidance in uncertain times.

As the kingdom of fire prepared to embrace its future under Kaen's reign, the echo of its victory and the promise of its encounter with the dragon resounded like an eternal flame, a reminder that even in the depths of the most difficult trials , the light of hope and courage would never be extinguished.

In the kingdoms where fire and water danced in an eternal choreography of creation and destruction, destiny wove its intricate web, uniting the lives of two beings marked by the will of the dragons. Kaen, newly crowned ruler of the kingdom of fire, invested with the power and wisdom of "The Wild One", and Fen, the warrior of water, blessed by "The Pacific" with the essence of the ocean, were on paths destined to converge. .

As each progressed on their own journey, facing trials and challenges that tested their courage and determination, a greater force pulled them toward a shared destiny. The war looming on the horizon, a storm wrought by ambition and the desire for power, threatened to shatter the balance the Six Dragons had fought so hard to maintain. Only together could Fen and Kaen face the approaching darkness and preserve the harmony of the world.

The story of Kaen, the enigmatic champion who emerged from the flames to lead his kingdom, and that of Fen, the brave fisherman transformed into the guardian of the water, were beginning to intertwine, woven together by the currents of destiny. The promise of their meeting echoed through the kingdoms, awakening both hope and fear in the hearts of those who understood the meaning of their union.

While Kaen consolidated his power and prepared his people for the uncertain times ahead, Fen continued his own quest for justice and truth, driven by the force of the water that flowed through his veins. Although their paths had not yet crossed, the wind of history blew with the promise of their inevitable meeting.

The world watched and waited, aware that the fate of Fen and Kaen was not theirs alone, but that of all beings that inhabited the realms. Together, they would face challenges that would test not only their strength and skill, but also the depth of their courage and the steadfastness of their spirit.

This prelude to the meeting of destiny marked the beginning of a new saga in the history of the kingdoms of fire and water, a saga of heroism, sacrifice and the tireless search for peace. The coming war would be a definitive test of the will of dragons and men, a confrontation whose outcome would define the future of the world.

As Fen and Kaen advanced toward their destination, the horizon was tinted with the colors of dawn, heralding the dawn of an era of challenges and hope. History was about to write a new chapter, one in which fire and water, instead of annihilating each other, would come together to forge a common destiny.

Chapter VI: Fen's Journey to the Kingdom of Fire

The path that Fen took towards the kingdom of fire was marked by the determination and the weight of the mission he had imposed on himself. Consumed by a whirlwind of emotions, where fury and sadness intermingled with the resolve to seek justice, Fen advanced through landscapes that changed with each step, each telling the story of a world that was delicately balanced between chaos and harmony.

The journey was long and lonely, a reflection of Fen's own inner path. He crossed vast plains that stretched under an immense sky, crossed ancient forests where the rustling of the leaves seemed to speak of ancient legends, and negotiated mountains whose peaks touched the clouds, defiant and majestic. With each step, Fen felt how the power of water granted by "The Pacific" strengthened him, not only physically, but also in his conviction to face whatever was necessary to reveal the truth.

As he approached the kingdom of fire, the air became warmer, and the sky took on shades of red and orange, as if the very flames of the kingdom welcomed him. The lands under his dominion shone with a fiery radiance, a landscape forged in the fire and passion of those who inhabited it. However, for Fen, each step towards this realm was a step towards the confrontation he knew he must have.

His arrival did not go unnoticed; The guards at the gates of the kingdom observed with curiosity and caution this traveler whose presence seemed to defy the very heat of the place. Fen, his gaze fixed on his destination, moved forward without hesitation, driven by the need for answers that had led him to cross worlds.

Heading directly to the palace where Kaen, the new ruler and champion of the kingdom of fire, resided, Fen prepared for the encounter that could change the course of his quest. The palace, a fortress of stone and flame, stood imposingly, reflecting the power and majesty of the kingdom it ruled.

As Fen delved deeper into the heart of the realm of fire, his determination grew stronger. He knew that the path he had chosen would not be easy, that the answers he sought might not be the ones he expected to find. However, he also knew that there was no turning back. The confrontation with Kaen, although uncertain in its outcome, was the inevitable next step in his journey towards the truth.

The first meeting between Fen and Kaen, two souls marked by destiny and transformed by the power of dragons, was about to happen. A meeting that could unite them in a common cause or pit them against each other in a conflict that would echo across the realms. As Fen advanced through the halls of the palace, fate awaited, ready to reveal its next move on the great board of history.

In the beating heart of the kingdom of fire, within the stone walls that had witnessed countless stories of power, valor and betrayal, Fen and Kaen finally met face to face. It was a moment that fate had woven with threads of fire and water, an encounter that would echo in the annals of the history of both kingdoms.

Fen, bearer of the power of the Water Dragon, entered the royal chambers with the weight of tragedy and determination marking his step. In front of him, Kaen, ruler of the kingdom of fire, recent victor of the Fire Tournament, emanated an authority and power that spoke of his recent encounter with "The Wild One". In the air between them, a palpable tension wove, charged with the power of the elements each represented.

Upon seeing each other, both warriors immediately felt each other's strength. Fen, with the freshness and depth of the ocean reflected in his eyes, and Kaen, whose gaze burned with the intensity and passion of fire. It was a moment of mutual recognition, not only of their strength, but also of the circumstances that had led them to this point.

Fen, with a voice that resonated with the force of the tides, stated his demand. He spoke of the tragedy that had devastated his life, of his search for justice and of the accusations that had brought him to the gates of the kingdom of fire. Every word was imbued with the fiery determination that characterized him, a call to truth and righteousness.

Kaen, for his part, listened with a serenity that contrasted with the storm that was raging inside him. Fen's accusations took him by surprise, denying them with the firmness of someone who knows the truth of his kingdom. He affirmed with conviction that no alliance with the kingdom of earth had stained the hands of fire, that the power and sovereignty of the kingdom he now ruled were incomparable and unbreakable.

The tension between the two reached its peak, a clash of wills and truths that seemed impossible to reconcile. Kaen, in a move that spoke both of his responsibility and his desire to protect his people from unnecessary conflict, made the decision to end the meeting. He ordered his guards to expel Fen from the palace, an act that sealed, for now, the distance between their worlds.

Fen, driven by the strength of his convictions, resisted with the fierce determination that had driven him across kingdoms in search of answers. But Kaen's order was unappealable, and the guards, faithful to their sovereign, complied without hesitation.

Thus, the destined meeting between Fen and Kaen concluded, not with a resolution, but with an even deeper chasm between them. Each returned to his element, carrying with him the certainty of his own truth and the uncertainty of what the future would hold. The war on the horizon seemed more inevitable now than ever, a conflict that would test not only their power, but also the delicate balance the Six Dragons had sworn to protect.

In an act of desperation and determination, Fen returned to the palace of the fire kingdom, his presence now marked by unwavering resolve. His demand echoed through the halls with the force of thunder, a cry that demanded a conference with "The Wild One" personally, convinced that only the dragon's words could dispel the shadows of doubt and betrayal that clouded his mind.

Kaen, faced again by the intrepid Fen, maintained his position with the firmness of the rock that resists the onslaught of the waves. His refusal was blunt, an insurmountable wall in the face of Fen's demands. With sovereign authority, he ordered his guards to escort Fen out, urging him to withdraw peacefully and thus avoid an escalation of the conflict.

However, Fen, whose spirit had been tempered by tragedy and strengthened by the power of the Water Dragon, was unwilling to accept a second rejection. Patience and supplication gave way to action; With fierce determination, he unleashed the power of the water that coursed through his veins. What had begun as a demand for the truth became a display of force capable of breaking down the barriers placed in its path.

The guards, surprised by the sudden manifestation of power, found themselves overwhelmed by the tide unleashed by Fen. One after another, they were unable to hold their ground against the fury and dominance of the water that Fen controlled. Each wave, each torrent, sought not only to break through, but also to demonstrate the seriousness of his purpose and the depth of his determination.

Fen, with the path clear thanks to his victory over the guards, stood firm in the heart of the palace. His figure, drenched and resplendent with the power of water, was a living challenge to the authority of Kaen and the established order of the kingdom of fire. I had crossed a threshold, not only physical, but also symbolic; He was no longer simply a seeker of truth, but a warrior willing to fight for it.

In that critical moment, with the defeated guards at his feet and the tension between him and Kaen reaching a boiling point, Fen remained unwavering. Their challenge had been issued, a challenge that would echo in the annals of the kingdoms' history, marking the beginning of a confrontation whose flames threatened to consume everything in its path.

The confrontation between Fen and Kaen, two forces of nature embodied in warriors, unleashed a cataclysm that resonated beyond the walls of the royal palace. As the battle intensified, the elements under his command intertwined in a whirlwind of destruction, testimony to the collision between water and fire, pain and power.

The palace, once a symbol of the majesty and unbreakable power of the kingdom of fire, now trembled under the impact of their fight. Every crash, every explosion of energy between Fen and Kaen, sent shockwaves through its ancient stones, fracturing columns, collapsing ceilings, and setting tapestries that had witnessed centuries of history into flames.

The destruction was not limited to the palace. As the battle dragged on, unrest gripped the city. The citizens, awakened by the roar of battle and the sky illuminated by flashes of fire and water, gathered in the streets, watching with a mixture of amazement and fear. The power displayed by both combatants was a force that defied understanding, a reminder of the primordial power that had shaped the world.

Fen, driven by a torrent of emotions and the indomitable drive of his cause, faced each of Kaen's attacks with a determination that bordered on recklessness. Although his abilities were remarkable, Kaen's mastery over the element of fire presented a challenge that seemed to surpass his limits.

Kaen, for his part, moved with lethal grace, his attacks imbued with the fury and intensity of the hottest volcano. Every blow he dealt was charged with the intention of ending the fight, although deep down, a spark of respect for Fen's tenacity began to burn.

The clash between water and fire became a spectacle that dominated the night sky, painting it with colors of terrible beauty. The fight between Fen and Kaen was not just a battle for justice or honor; It had become a manifestation of the eternal struggle between opposing elements, a dance of creation and destruction unfolding before the eyes of the entire kingdom.

As the royal palace crumbled piece by piece under the weight of their confrontation, the question looming over everyone present was clear: what would be the outcome of this battle? What fate awaited the kingdom of fire and its inhabitants, witnesses of a conflict whose outcome could alter the balance of the world?

The answer, still hidden in the flames and waves that consumed the palace, remained elusive, suspended on the edge of each sword, in the heart of each wave. The city waited, holding its breath, as the future of its kingdom was decided in the heat of battle.

After hours of titanic combat, where fire and water clashed with a ferocity that resonated through the realm of fire, the battle between Fen and Kaen finally found its conclusion. The destruction they had left in their wake was a testament to the power and passion with which each warrior had fought, each driven by their convictions and the strength of the elements at their command.

As dawn began to color the sky with the first rays of light, a figure emerged victorious among the still smoldering ruins of the royal palace. Kaen, the ruler of the kingdom of fire, had proven to be the winner in this confrontation of ancient powers. His mastery over fire, combined with the skill and strategy honed along his path to the throne, had allowed him to surpass the formidable strength that Fen, blessed by the power of water, had displayed.

The final moment of the fight had been as intense as it was heartbreaking. Kaen, recognizing Fen's courage and determination, did not wish for a fatal outcome. However, responsibility towards his people and protecting the balance of the world prompted him to make a difficult decision. With a blow that concentrated all the essence of the fire he commanded, Kaen ended the fight, leaving Fen unconscious but alive.

Taking Fen in his arms, Kaen began the journey towards the outskirts of the kingdom, to the vast desert that stretched beyond the borders of fire. There, in the center of that sea of sand and loneliness, he left Fen, ensuring that, despite the defeat, he would have a chance to survive and perhaps, find his own path once again.

Kaen's decision to take Fen into the desert was not only an act of mercy, but also a recognition of the courage and strength Fen had shown. In the solitude of the desert, far from the kingdoms that had seen them clash, Kaen hoped that Fen could reflect on his journey and the truths he sought.

As Kaen returned alone to the realm of fire, the weight of the decisions made during the battle weighed on him. Although he had ensured the safety of his people and defended the honor of his kingdom, victory brought him no joy. He knew that the wounds opened during the confrontation would need time to heal, both in Fen's heart and in the very fabric of the world they had both sworn to protect.

The fire kingdom slowly began the rebuilding process, healing the scars left by the battle. Kaen, as its sovereign, pledged to lead this effort, guiding his people toward a future of peace and stability. Yet deep within, Kaen knew that the encounter with Fen had changed something fundamental in him, a transformation forged in the heat of battle, the consequences of which were yet to be discovered.

Chapter VII: Resurgence in the Desert

The sun rose relentlessly over the vast desert, turning the sky a fiery orange that reflected the intensity of the fire Fen had fought. His awakening was a moment of confusion and pain, a slow awareness of his loneliness in an endless sea of sand. The defeat at the hands of Kaen, far from breaking his spirit, had further fueled his determination to seek justice and answers.

Fen stood, feeling the weight of each wound, each bruise a testament to the confrontation that had taken place. However, these physical wounds were nothing compared to the steely determination that burned within him. Despite the initial disorientation, his will to continue his search remained unwavering.

He looked around, the desert stretched in all directions, a limitless horizon that challenged his perception of space and time. Fen knew that surviving this hostile environment would be a test of his resilience and cunning, but he was determined to overcome every obstacle. Every step he took in the hot sand was an affirmation of his willingness to move forward, a promise to himself that he would not let his defeat define his journey.

The loneliness of the desert, instead of plunging him into despair, became his companion in this new chapter of his search. The fury and sadness that had accompanied him until this moment were now mixed with renewed clarity. Fen understood that the battle against Kaen had been only one part of a greater challenge, a fragment of the truth that he had yet to unravel.

With each kilometer he covered, Fen grew stronger, not only physically, but also in his understanding of the world and himself. The adversity of the desert, with its extremes of heat during the day and cold at night, tempered his spirit, preparing him for what was to come.

Fen's fate remained uncertain, the road ahead filled with unanswered questions and unknown challenges. However, his determination to find the truth, to do justice for the loss he had suffered, remained unchanged. In the desert, far from everything he knew, Fen found a new strength, a resurgence of purpose that would carry him through the trials he still had to face.

As the sun set, painting the desert with long, deep shadows, Fen continued his march. His silhouette, a solitary figure against the vast canvas of the desert, was a symbol of resistance and hope. Fen's quest for truth and justice was far from over; In fact, it was just beginning.

Fen's search for answers and justice had taken him through desolate landscapes and harrowing confrontations, but no trial had been as challenging as the vast desert that now stretched before him. Every day, every step, became a fight for survival, a battle against the relentless nature that surrounded him and against the wounds that marked his body and spirit.

With each day, the hope of finding answers faded a little more, leaving in its place a bone-deep exhaustion. Fen, driven by a purpose that he could not abandon, continued on his way, but his strength was gradually leaving him. The abilities that "The

Pacific" had given him, now diminished by the lack of energy and the pain of his wounds, were not enough to sustain him.

Finally, after days of superhuman effort, Fen reached the limit of his endurance. In a last act of will, he tried to move forward, but his body did not respond. With a labored breath and his heart pounding desperately in his chest, he fell to the desert floor, the dust and sand caressing his face like a cold, indifferent bed.

In that moment of vulnerability, when the darkness began to close in on him, a silhouette appeared on the horizon. It was an almost ethereal presence, moving with a grace that defied the scorching heat and desolate vastness of the desert. The figure approached slowly, a point of light in the immensity of the sunset.

Fen, struggling to stay conscious, tried to focus his sights on the approaching figure. Was it a mirage, a last mockery of his exhausted mind? Or was it someone, or something, who had been sent to guide him or, perhaps, to finish what the battle with Kaen had started?

Before he could find the answers to his questions, exhaustion and pain completely overcame him, plunging him into darkness. Fen fainted, leaving his fate in the hands of the mysterious figure who, against all hope, had appeared at his most desperate moment.

The desert, silent witness of this encounter, jealously guarded its secrets. As night fell over the sand, the silhouette stood beside the fallen warrior, gazing with a gaze that spoke of ancient knowledge and mysteries yet to be revealed. Fen's story, far from ending in that desolate place, was about to take a new turn, guided by the hand of a stranger whose intentions remained hidden in the shadows of twilight.

The mysterious figure that approached Fen in his most desperate moment turned out to be Aria, a noble maiden from the kingdom of air. This kingdom, known for its vast grasslands that changed with the wind and its ever-moving skies, was a place of ethereal beauty and unfathomable powers. Unlike other kingdoms, the air did not have a single ruler; Instead, a set of noble families shared control, maintaining a delicate balance of power through alliances and agreements.

Belonging to one of these venerable families, Aria was known not only for her lineage but also for her deep connection to the element of air. From an early age, he had demonstrated an exceptional affinity with currents and winds, an ability that had earned him the respect and admiration of his people. However, Aria longed for more than just life at court; Her adventurous spirit led her to explore beyond the borders of her kingdom, seeking to better understand the world and her place in it.

It was on one of these exploratory trips that Aria found Fen, fallen and near death in the desert. Moved by an innate sense of compassion and curiosity for the stranger who had come so far from the domains of water, she decided to rescue him. Using his wind-bending abilities, he carefully transported it across the desert, bringing it to the safety of the realm of air.

The kingdom of air was a place of constant change, where the great grasslands transformed with every breeze and every storm. Here, power did not reside in a throne, but was dispersed among the numerous noble families, each with its own history, its own allies and rivals. These families, through generations of diplomacy and sometimes conflict, had learned to coexist, maintaining the peace and stability of the kingdom.

In extraordinary circumstances, noble families could request the intervention of "The Changeling", the guardian dragon of the air, whose presence was as elusive as the wind itself. Although "The Changeling" did not always respond to these calls, his wisdom and power were a valuable resource to the kingdom, used only in times of great need.

Aria, with her act of saving Fen, had drawn a new link between the realms of water and air, a bridge between worlds that rarely met. While Fen rested, recovering from his wounds in Aria's abode, the kingdom of air prepared to receive this unexpected visitor, whose arrival could mean the beginning of a new alliance or the harbinger of even greater challenges.

The noble maiden, in her decision to help Fen, had not only shown the goodness of her heart, but also the vision of a leader who saw beyond the borders of her own world. In the shifting grasslands of the kingdom of air, Fen would find not only refuge and healing, but also a new direction in his search for justice and truth.

Fen opened his eyes slowly, fighting the confusion and disorientation that enveloped him like a thick fog. The last thing he remembered was the desolate immensity of the desert, the suffocating heat on his skin and an overwhelming feeling of defeat. Now, however, he found himself in a completely different place, a room whose walls and furniture were completely foreign to him.

The soft light filtering through the windows bathed the room in a serene calm, a stark contrast to the chaos and violence of his last memories. Fen tried to get up, but his body responded with a dull ache, a reminder of the physical trials he had faced. However, he noticed that his wounds had been treated, his skin healed from the abrasions and cuts he had suffered.

As he tried to gather his thoughts and understand his situation, the door to the room opened softly. Through the threshold entered a figure that seemed to move with the grace and lightness of the wind itself. It was Aria, the noble maiden of the kingdom of air, whose presence in the room filled the space with a calm and comforting energy.

Aria approached Fen with a look full of curiosity and concern. Fen, still trying to process his surroundings and enhanced state, took a moment to respond. Confusion was palpable in his voice as he finally articulated his thoughts, asking in turn how he had been saved and brought to this unknown place.

With patience and a kind smile, Aria told him how she had found him passed out in the desert, how she had felt the urge to help him, and how she had carried him through the air currents to the safety of her home in the kingdom of the air. His story was fascinating, a story of compassion and bravery that resonated deep within Fen, who listened attentively, taking in every word.

As Aria finished her explanation, the atmosphere in the room became more intimate, marked by a tacit understanding of shared vulnerability. It was then that Aria, with a look that reflected a mix of interest and genuine concern, asked the question that was weighing on his mind: "What happened to you to end up in that place and in that state?"

Now Fen, faced with Aria's question, on the threshold of sharing his story, a narrative of loss, search and determination. This encounter, marked by unexpected kindness and the opportunity for a new beginning, promises to be the beginning of a deep and meaningful connection between two souls united by fate in the vast and ever-changing realm of air.

Sitting face to face, the room illuminated by the soft light coming through the windows, Fen began to tell his story to Aria. The noble maiden of the air listened attentively, her gaze fixed on Fen, as he unraveled the thread of events that had led him to this moment.

Fen spoke of the life he had led before, an existence marked by simplicity and love, living in harmony with the Pacific kingdom. He described the fateful day when everything changed, when a fiery meteor, covered in magma, devastated his home and took away what he loved most in the world: his wife and son. The tragedy was the catalyst that awakened in him a thirst for justice, a burning desire to find those responsible and make them pay for their actions.

He continued to recount his journey, the way his search for answers had led him to confront the kingdom of fire. He explained how he had been defeated and banished by Kaen, the ruler of the kingdom of fire, despite his demand for justice and his right to confront "The Wild One" for answers.

Aria, the last of a noble lineage that had ruled the lands of the air since ancient times, listened to Fen's story with deep empathy. Despite the greatness of her heritage, there was a humility and capacity for compassion that distinguished her. He understood the pain and despair Fen felt, for in his own veins ran the blood of those who had served and protected the kingdom of air with honor and sacrifice.

As Fen shared the details of his fight and his motivations, Aria reflected on the weight of history and the implications of the battle Fen had fought. The nobility of his cause, his fight against adversity and injustice, resonated with the principles that governed the kingdom of the air: the search for balance, justice and the protection of the innocent.

Fen's confession not only served as an outlet for his wounded soul, but also as a bridge between two worlds that rarely met. Aria, moved by Fen's story and aware of the role her lineage played in guarding the principles of air, found herself faced with a crucial decision. The connection forged between them in that moment of vulnerability and sincerity promised to be the beginning of an unexpected alliance, a union of forces between water and air against the injustices that Fen sought to rectify.

Aria contemplates how to respond to Fen's story, how to help him in his quest, and what role she, as an air noble, might play in the fight for justice and balance. In the heart of the kingdom of air, two souls had found common ground, prepared to face together the challenges that destiny had in store for them.

Aria's determination to help Fen brought her to a challenge that few in the realm of air would have dared to face. His lineage, although noble and ancient, had been the object of contempt by the other noble families, who saw in his free spirit and his empathy towards others a departure from the traditions that governed their high spheres. However, Aria, moved by unwavering conviction, decided to take a bold action: request an audience with "The Changeling", the elusive Dragon of Air, on behalf of Fen and her cause.

Aria's request was not initially well received. Going to "The Changeling" was an act reserved for times of great need, and noble families viewed with suspicion any attempt to influence the dragon's designs. However, Aria, armed with the strength of her purpose and the urgency of the situation, managed to convince the noble families of the importance of her request. But this victory was not without conditions.

The noble families, in a gesture that mixed their desire to maintain the status quo with their distrust of Aria, agreed to her request under one drastic condition: she would have to renounce her title of nobility. This sacrifice, a price to pay for the help he sought, was a testament to the weight of traditions and power wielded by noble families in the kingdom of the air.

Aria, faced with the choice of whether to adhere to convention or follow the calling of her heart, did not hesitate. With his gaze fixed on a future where justice for Fen could be achieved, he accepted the conditions imposed. His renunciation of the title was not only an act of personal selflessness, but also a declaration of his values, a testimony to his commitment to causes greater than the privileges of his birth.

Now, all Aria and Fen could do was wait for "The Changeling" to return from his usual flights. There was no certainty that the dragon would grant their request or even grant them an audience. However, Aria remained firm in her decision, sustained by the hope that her sacrifice would not be in vain.

During that time of waiting, Fen made a full recovery under Aria's care. His body healed and his spirit grew stronger, thanks not only to the medicine and shelter he was given in the realm of air, but also to the bond that had been forged between him and the noble maiden. Aria's nobility of heart and their shared understanding of pain and loss allowed them to connect on a deep level, preparing them for the encounter with "The Changeling" and the challenges that were yet to come.

During the days Fen spent recovering in the realm of air, not only did his physical wounds heal, but his spirit also found solace and strength. Aria's story, her sacrifice and the firmness with which she stood up to her own kingdom for helping a foreigner, had a profound impact on Fen. The nobility of his actions, giving up his title and facing the disdain of the other noble families, offered Fen a different perspective on courage and dedication. It was not just the battle on the field that defined a person's worth, but also the sacrifices made in the name of ideals and justice.

This time of reflection and deep conversations with Aria strengthened the bond between them, forging an unbreakable friendship based on mutual respect and shared understanding of personal losses and battles. Aria shared with Fen the stories of her kingdom, the traditions of the air, and taught him to appreciate the beauty in the constant change that defined their home.

When news of "The Changeling's" return arrived, Fen felt renewed, not only physically, but also in his determination to face what was to come. Aria, for her part, remained by his side, becoming not only his guide but also his ally in the search for justice.

Together, they began the journey towards the domains of the Air Dragon, a journey marked by the uncertainty of what they would find. Aria had given up a lot to facilitate this meeting, and they both knew there were no guarantees that "The Changeling" would agree to help them. However, hope and the need for answers drove them forward.

The path to the dragon's abode was a reflection of the kingdom of air itself: changing, full of fleeting beauties and unexpected challenges. Aria and Fen, moving through grasslands that transformed with each gust of wind, felt the majesty of the air enveloping them, reminding them of the strength and freedom that this element represented.

Upon arriving at the domain of "The Changeling", they found themselves before a vastness that seemed to touch the sky itself. There, where the air currents converged and danced in an ethereal spectacle, they waited for the dragon to appear, prepared to face their destiny.

Now with Aria and Fen, standing before the immensity of the air, contemplating the horizon where the sky met the earth. This moment of calm before the storm symbolized not only the end of one journey, but also the beginning of another. Before them, the possibility of a conference with "The Changeling" unfolded, a meeting that could change the course of their struggle and, perhaps, the destiny of the world.

In the heart of the Air Dragon's domain, Aria and Fen stood before "The Changeling", whose imposing presence defied mortal comprehension. Aria, with her characteristic grace and determination, formally requested a conference for Fen, highlighting the importance of her request and the urgency of her cause.

Initially, the dragon showed reluctance. Intervention in mortal matters was an action he did not take lightly, aware of the consequences his decisions could have on the delicate balance of the world. However, the mention of Aria's sacrifice, her willingness to give up her nobility for Fen's quest for justice, caught the dragon's attention. This act of selflessness and willpower resonated with "The Changeling", who saw in it a reflection of the principles that governed the kingdom of air: change, adaptability, and sacrifice for the greater good.

Moved by the exceptional circumstances and Aria's conviction, "The Changeling" agreed to grant the hearing. Fen, aware of the unique opportunity presented to him, came forward to share his story with the guardian of the air. He narrated the events that had marked his life from the tragedy that had led him to undertake his search, to the confrontation with Kaen in the kingdom of fire and his subsequent banishment to the desert.

Fen's story, told with sincerity and emotion, resonated in the vast space, capturing the dragon's attention. "The Changeling" listened, his ethereal presence fluctuating with each word, as if the currents of air themselves carried Fen's narrative across the confines of his realm.

As he concluded his story, a deep silence filled the room. Fen, along with Aria, waited with bated breath, aware that the dragon's response could mean a decisive change in their fight for justice. "The Changeling", after reflecting on what he had heard, spoke with a voice that resonated like the wind across the mountains. He agreed to not only recognize Fen's sacrifice and determination but also offer his blessing, a gesture of support that, while not involving direct intervention, set a precedent in the relationship between the elemental kingdoms and mortal causes.

With Fen and Aria receiving the blessing of the Air Dragon, a moment of hope and renewed determination. The conference with "The Changeling" had been a success, not only because of the audience granted but because of the recognition of the value of his cause. With the wind at his back and the blessing of an ancient dragon, Fen prepared to face the next challenges on his path to justice, knowing now that he was not alone in his fight.

The moment of the blessing bestowed by "The Changeling" was one of power and promise, a turning point for Fen in his quest for justice. However, the audience with the Air Dragon also brought with it warnings and conditions that Fen and Aria had to accept and understand in their full magnitude.

"The Changeling", his voice resounding like the echo of a distant wind, made it clear to Fen that, though his cause was just and his heart brave, direct intervention in the affairs of mortals was beyond his capabilities. The reason for this limitation lay in the delicate balance that governed the world, a balance that even the guardian dragons were forced to respect. The help given to Fen, in the form of a blessing, was a gesture of moral and spiritual support, but not a direct intervention in his conflict.

Aria, who had listened carefully to the interaction between Fen and the dragon, was thrown into her own dilemma when "The Changeling" addressed her directly. Despite her bravery and willingness to accompany Fen on her journey, the dragon had other plans for the noble maiden. Aria, whose sacrifice and determination had been crucial to gaining the audience, found herself faced with a new task assigned by "The Changeling".

The dragon revealed to him that his path did not continue with Fen, but in the kingdom of air, where he was required for a mission of vital importance. Although the details were veiled and mysterious, the dragon's solemn tone indicated the gravity of the task. Aria, whose heart had been committed to supporting Fen, felt a mixture of surprise and regret at the news. However, the realization that each individual had a role to play in the grand design of the world helped her accept the decision with grace and determination.

The promise of support to Fen was now transformed into a blessing from a distance, while Aria faced her own journey, a path that would lead her to explore unknown depths of her being and the kingdom of air. Although their destinies seemed to diverge, the bond forged between them would remain, an indelible bond forged in mutual respect and the shared struggle for a more just world.

With a heavy heart but an unbreakable spirit, Fen prepared to continue his journey, now alone, but carrying with him the blessing of the Air Dragon and the memory of Aria's nobility.

Aria's departure was not a goodbye, but a see you later, in a world where the paths of the brave are destined to cross again.

The chapter concludes with Fen emerging from the dragon's domain, looking toward the horizon with a renewed sense of purpose. He knew that the challenges he would face would be arduous, but the strength and hope he had found in the realm of air gave him the courage to face whatever came. Fen's journey continued, a lonely path toward truth and justice, illuminated by the star of a destiny yet to be revealed.

Chapter VIII: In the Firm Lands

Fen, with the determination that characterized him, began the journey towards the kingdom of earth in search of "The Firm One", the Dragon of the Earth. This kingdom, known for its vast expanse of agricultural fields and deep mines, was a place where people lived in harmony with the land, cultivating its fruits and excavating its secrets.

From the moment he crossed the borders of this robust kingdom, Fen witnessed a life shaped by the hard work of its inhabitants. Despite the beauty of the landscape, with its towering mountains and fertile valleys, a sense of defiance permeated the air. The kingdom's inhabitants, though friendly, were deeply entrenched in their daily tasks, focused on farming and mining, and unwilling or unable to provide information about the legendary dragon's whereabouts.

Every day, Fen walked through towns and villages, asking about "The Firm One" from anyone who seemed old enough or looked enough to know the ancient legends. However, his questions were often met with confused looks or evasive answers. It seemed that for many, "The Firm One" was just a character from the tales of yesteryear, an echo of a bygone era that was fading in the collective memory.

As her attempts to find concrete clues failed again and again, Fen began to feel the weight of her mission. His frustration grew with each unsatisfactory answer, each incomplete story about the dragon that had once dominated the land with its colossal strength. It was evident that the connection between the dragons and the people of the kingdom had faded over time, leaving behind only vestiges of the truths they once knew.

Reflecting on his situation, Fen decided to change his approach. Instead of searching directly for "The Firm One", he dedicated himself to exploring the most remote areas of the kingdom, those regions where legends still maintained their magic and the passage of time seemed to move at a different pace. He ventured beyond the cultivated fields and bustling mines, toward the mountains where the ancients said dragons used to retreat.

It was on these explorations that Fen finally encountered an elderly miner at the end of his work day. The man, whose face was marked by the wrinkles of a millennium of stories, told him about a specific mountain that housed phenomena that no other place in the kingdom presented. Intrigued and revitalized by this new information, Fen felt he was close to his goal.

Reinforced by the miner's guidance, Fen adjusted his course towards the aforementioned mountain. With each step towards this new destination, his hope was renewed. Perhaps, after so much searching, he was finally on the threshold of finding "The Firm One" and, with him, the answers he so longed to discover. Fen's journey continued, taking him closer to the truth, towards the heart of the earth's kingdom.

Upon reaching the foothills of the imposing mountain, Fen felt a mixture of disappointment and amazement. Despite the expectations that had accompanied him on his path, the mountain itself did not reveal any obvious signs of the presence of a dragon. However, the land around the mountain throbbed with unusual richness, the nearby mines were prosperous and emanated an energy that resonated with the echo of ancient powers.

As Fen contemplated the landscape, trying to decipher the mysteries of the mountain, he met Einar, a young miner whose curiosity had led him to follow in Fen's footsteps since his arrival in the earth kingdom. Einar, with an inquisitive spirit and a bright gaze of excitement, approached Fen not only out of fascination with the stranger, but also out of the resonance of his own quest for knowledge.

"Einar introduced himself with a mixture of respect and frank curiosity," Fen later described. The young miner had heard Fen speak in the taverns and markets, where the foreigner asked for "The Firm One". Moved by Fen's persistence and her story, Einar decided to offer his help.

"The lands around this mountain have always been rich, beyond normal," Einar explained as they walked together towards the most accessible bases of the mountain. "My grandfather told me that this prosperity has its roots in a very ancient legend, which speaks of "The Firm One" resting in the heart of the mountain. No one has actually seen the dragon, but the land seems blessed by its presence."

Einar also revealed that he had recently heard a story from an old miner, who spoke of how the subtle vibrations and richness of the mines could be linked to a dragon's blessing. "It is as if the mountain breathes very gently, and with each breath, it enriches everything around it," he added with a tone of reverence.

Upon hearing these words, Fen felt a bond with the blessing he had received from "The Changeling". Einar's description of the mountain breathing and enriching the earth resonated with what the air dragon had hinted about its own subtle but powerful influence. Motivated by this new understanding and Einar's help, Fen decided to explore the mountain further in search of the legendary "The Firm One".

Fen and Einar prepare to enter the mountain at dawn the next day, full of renewed hope and determination. The adventure ahead promised discoveries and perhaps an encounter with the elusive Earth Dragon, a long-awaited chapter in Fen's long quest for justice and truth.

The journey to the heart of the mountain was not easy. Fen and Einar faced narrow passages and dark paths, where each step seemed to resonate with an ancient echo. The atmosphere inside the mountain was dense, loaded with a history that felt engraved in the stones themselves.

As they advanced, they encountered natural obstacles: deep crevices that had to be crossed carefully and dislodged rocks that threatened to block their path. Despite these challenges, Fen's determination never wavered; Buoyed by the promise of answers, he continued forward with Einar at his side, who shared his enthusiasm and respect for the magnitude of his surroundings.

Finally, after hours of descending, they reached a vast underground chamber. The place was impressive, dominated by a colossal statue carved directly into the rock of the mountain. The statue of "The Firm One" was majestic, evoking the strength and power of the Earth Dragon. Despite its inert form, the energy of the place was palpable, as if the dragon's essence still permeated the air.

As Fen approached the statue, a gentle breeze unusual in the stagnant underground air blew through the chamber. This light wind seemed like a whisper from "The Changeling", a subtle but clear sign that Fen was on the right path. Inspired by this sign, Fen began to relate his story to the statue, speaking as if "The Firm One" could hear him.

Fen shared every detail of her journey: the loss of her family, her search for justice, the challenges faced, and the revelations found. He expressed his need to understand the truth behind the alliance between the kingdoms of fire and earth, and his hope to restore the balance that had been disturbed by such actions.

As Fen spoke, the atmosphere in the chamber seemed to change, the breeze becoming more present, fluttering around the statue as if picking up Fen's every word. It was a moment of deep communion, a silent dialogue between Fen and the dragon legacy that was said to rest in that place.

While Fen and Einar silently contemplated, waiting for some response or sign from "The Firm One" The story of Fen, deposited in the heart of the mountain, was now intertwined with the legend of the Earth Dragon, hoping to awaken the ancient force that could help restore justice and balance to the world.

The underground chamber, a place of mysteries and legends, became the scene of a shocking revelation when the statue representing "The Firm One" began to crack. Cracks multiplied rapidly across the stone surface, breaking off pieces that crashed to the ground with dull crashes. Before the disbelieving eyes of Fen and Einar, the statue crumbled completely, revealing the imposing figure of the Earth Dragon.

"The Firm One" emerged not as the wise and ancient guardian Fen had imagined, but as an unleashed and furious force of nature. His body was a mosaic of rock and earth, vibrant with a power that seemed ripped straight from the core of the world. With a roar that echoed through the depths of the mountain, the dragon expressed its anger, shaking the ground and causing stones the size of houses to begin to fall around the chamber.

Fen, despite the imminent danger, attempted to communicate with the dragon. "I have come seeking understanding, not confrontation!" Fen yelled at the dragon, hoping to calm its uncontrollable rage. But "The Firm One" showed no signs of having listened or wanting to listen. His fury seemed fueled by deeper, older grievances, and his only response was to intensify the assault, striking the ground with such force that he seemed to want to tear the mountain itself apart.

Einar, grabbing Fen's arm, shouted above the chaos, "We must leave, now!" There was no time for more attempts at dialogue. Together, they began a desperate race toward the exit, dodging falling debris and cracks opening beneath their feet. The entire structure of the mountain seemed to be collapsing, as if the dragon's very presence was undoing the integrity of the place.

As they ran, the sound of the mountain crumbling amplified around them, a cacophony of destruction that resonated with the Earth Dragon's wrath. Every step they took was fraught with danger, every look back showed them the extent of the destructive power of "The Firm One".

With Fen and Einar barely ahead of the wave of destruction, their escape is a race against the unstoppable force of nature unleashed. Behind them, the mountain became a tomb of stone and dust, sealing what had been the sanctuary of "The Firm One" and leaving a testament to the devastating strength of the angry dragon.

After a harrowing escape through the ruined corridors of the mountain, Fen and Einar emerged outside just as the last part of the structure collapsed in a thunderous crash. Behind them, what was once an imposing shrine was now nothing more than a pile of rubble and dust, testimony to the destructive power of "The Firm One".

Exhausted but alive, they both paused for a moment to catch their breath, looking back at the smoldering ruins. The air was filled with dense dust that blocked the sunlight, creating an artificial twilight around the place where they had narrowly escaped their stone tomb.

Einar, his face marked with dust and worry, turned to Fen with a grave expression. "I need to go back to town and gather our people," he said with determination. "The Firm One" has been the guardian of this kingdom for generations, and his fury today may have spread fear and despair. I must make sure everyone is safe and understand what has happened here."

Fen nodded, understanding Einar's responsibility to his people. "Your duty is to them," he replied, putting a hand on the young miner's shoulder. "And mine leads me to continue searching for answers, to continue this journey until I discover the truth behind all this chaos."

The conversation between the two, although brief, was a clear reflection of their divergent paths. Einar, his heart tied to his home and community, was preparing to lead in a time of crisis, while Fen, driven by a burning desire for justice and answers, felt compelled to move forward.

"Thank you for everything, Einar," Fen said, extending his hand in a gesture of camaraderie. "Without your help, I might not have survived the secrets of that mountain."

Einar returned the gesture, with a sad but proud smile. "And I owe my life to you, Fen. Go and find your answers. I hope that when we meet again, we both have good news to share."

With those final words, Einar headed towards the valley, towards the town that now more than ever needed his presence and leadership. Fen, for his part, adjusted his backpack and looked towards the horizon, towards the kingdom of fire, where he felt the answers he was looking for were heading.

As Fen walked away from the still-smoldering ruins of the earth kingdom, his mind was troubled by images of the dragon unleashing its uncontrollable fury. The devastating strength of "The Firm One" had left an indelible impression on him, clearly showing that, in his current state, he was not prepared to directly face the power of a dragon.

The reality of his own vulnerability led him to an inescapable conclusion: he needed to strengthen himself, not only physically but also in mastering the powers that now resided within him, courtesy of the Water Dragon. Furthermore, the Earth Dragon's inexplicable fury raised a question that could not be left unanswered. What had provoked such rage in such a powerful creature? The answer, Fen suspected, could be found where it all began: his home in the Pacific kingdom.

Determined, Fen plotted a new course of action. Before facing any other threat or seeking more allies among the dragons, he must return to his home village, to the exact spot where the meteor had struck and set off the chain of events that now consumed him. He needed to fully understand every detail of that fateful day, review the ruins, look for clues he had initially overlooked, and above all, evaluate any changes that may have occurred since his departure.

With these reflections marking his course, Fen crossed the borders of the earth kingdom. His figure was silhouetted against the vast horizon, a lonely traveler in search of power and truth. He knew that each step brought him closer to future confrontations, but also to the answers he needed to restore peace and balance to his world.

The chapter concludes with Fen walking alone, his silhouette receding from the crumbling mountain, heading towards the Pacific realm. As he set out on the familiar paths of his youth, determination and resolve shone in his eyes. He was ready to face whatever was necessary, armed with the resilience and wisdom gained from his confrontations and discoveries. His journey, although full of challenges, was also a path of rediscovery and hope, always taking him forward, towards the heart of his own story.

Chapter IX: Preparations in the Kingdom of Fire

In the vibrant kingdom of fire, under the rule of Kaen, a new palace had risen from the ashes of the old one, destroyed during his confrontation with Fen. This new building was an architectural marvel that reflected both the strength and cunning of its sovereign. Built from the strongest volcanic rocks and adorned with obsidian that glistened in the hot sun, the palace stood like an imposing fortress on a cliff overlooking the vast volcanic landscape.

The design of the palace incorporated dynamic elements that personified the element of fire. Tall, thin towers, resembling petrified flames, reached into the sky, while walls and balconies were designed to capture and reflect sunlight, creating a glow that could be seen from miles away. The heart of the palace housed a vast throne room, where a wrought iron throne, encrusted with gems that mimicked embers, served as Kaen's center of power.

However, the architectural marvel was abruptly interrupted by the looming threat. Kaen, while overseeing the latest additions to the palace, felt a deep tremor that resonated through the ground, a vibration so powerful that it could only mean one thing: the arrival of "The Firm One" Quickly, he climbed to the highest of the towers to look out over the horizon and there he saw it, an earth dragon, wrapped in an aura of anger, flying directly towards the kingdom of fire.

Aware of the danger that "The Firm One" represented not only for him but for his entire kingdom, Kaen acted with the decision that characterized him. He immediately ordered the evacuation of all the inhabitants of the palace and began to prepare the city's defenses. His voice resonated with authority and calm through the palace's magical communication system, urging everyone to seek shelter and prepare for a possible confrontation.

"Mobilize defenses, prepare elemental shields, and evacuate the citizens to the caverns of refuge," he ordered his captains. Meanwhile, his closest advisors gathered around him, bringing maps and contingency plans.

The kingdom of fire mobilized as a single entity, with an efficiency and speed forged in countless past battles and challenges. The streets were filled with citizens who, although accustomed to heat and fire, were not prepared to face the fury of a dragon as powerful as "The Firm One"

Kaen standing on the palace's tallest tower, his silhouette silhouetted dramatically against the twilight sky. His eyes never strayed from the enormous dragon that was rapidly approaching, a mass of fury and elemental power. As the hot wind whipped across his face, the determination and gravity of his position as sovereign had never been clearer. The kingdom of fire was preparing for an encounter that could define its future, with Kaen at the forefront, ready to face the approaching storm.

The arrival of "The Firm One" at the newly built palace of Kaen was as dramatic as it was feared. As the towering earth dragon approached, the sky above the kingdom of fire seemed to darken with its presence, and a series of minor tremors anticipated its landing. The flames of the torches in the palace flickered under the influence of its powerful aura, while guards and servants rushed to secure the fortifications and evacuate the most exposed areas.

Despite the palpable tension and the dragon's intimidating presence, Kaen maintained his composure. He stood firmly on the great balcony of the palace, hoping to confront the dragon, not with weapons, but with words.

When "The Firm One" landed with a crash that echoed through the palace courtyard, its size and strength were overwhelming. Despite his fury, he initiated a conversation, demanding an immediate conference with ""The Wild One". "I must talk to him, not a human," he growled in a tone that echoed like an earthquake.

Kaen, although aware of his disadvantaged position, tried to negotiate. "Allow me to be the mediator between you," he proposed, trying to control the situation and possibly hide details that he preferred not to reveal directly to "The Firm One" "I can assure that your message will reach "The Wild One" without the need for a direct encounter."

However, "The Firm One" spurned the offer with a contemptuous roar. "You, Kaen, are nothing more than a pawn in this power game. "The Wild One" must hear the truth from my own lips, and I will tolerate no intermediaries." Their stance was uncompromising, and with each word, the ground beneath them vibrated with their growing irritation.

The last warning from "The Firm One" made it clear that there was no room for more negotiations. "This is your last chance to comply without consequences," he warned, his voice so loud it almost made the palace windows vibrate.

Kaen retreated inside his palace, his mind agitated by the dilemma he faced. On the one hand, he wanted to protect his kingdom and maintain control over the situation; On the other hand, "The Firm One's" insistence on speaking directly to "The Wild One" threatened to unravel secrets that Kaen had fought to keep hidden. As he watched the earth dragon from a high window, his expression was a mix of determination and worry, knowing that the decisions he made next could alter the fate of his entire kingdom.

"The Firm One's" patience quickly ran out, and without further ado, he unleashed his fury against Kaen. With a roar that shook the foundations of the palace, the earth dragon struck the ground with such force that a crack formed that stretched across the courtyard, sending debris and sparks in all directions.

Kaen, standing in front of the towering dragon, showed no signs of fear. As the first shockwave of earth and stone headed towards him, he raised a hand in a gesture of authority and with a low murmur, the wave dissipated before it could reach him. The crowd watching from safety couldn't believe it; Not only had Kaen parried the attack, he did so with disconcerting ease.

"Enough!" Kaen shouted firmly, his voice resonating with a power that seemed to rival that of the dragon. "I do not wish to fight you. Not here, not now."

However, "The Firm One", incited by his own anger and perhaps the lack of fear in Kaen, intensified his attacks. Its paws hit the ground, sending waves of dirt towards the palace. He lifted huge boulders and hurled them with devastating force towards Kaen, each with enough power to demolish an entire section of the palace.

But Kaen, with unearthly calm, extended his hand each time, and the rocks disintegrated into the air, reduced to nothing more than dust before they could touch him. His ability to repel attacks was amazing, and with each successful defense, "The Firm One's" frustration grew.

The battle between them became a spectacle of ancient and modern powers, a clash of earth and fire that illuminated the sky of the kingdom of fire with flashes of elemental energy. Kaen, moving with an agility and precision that defied his human appearance, avoided the dragon's direct attacks, responding with barriers of fire and controlled explosions that neutralized "The Firm One's" offensive.

With each exchange, it became clearer that Kaen possessed abilities beyond anything anyone in the kingdom had witnessed. His stamina and ability to restrain a raging dragon were evidence of a power that few, if any, humans had ever achieved.

With "The Firm One", exhausted and surprised, stepping back momentarily, his heavy breath forming clouds of steam in the hot air. Kaen, still unfazed, remained standing, his figure illuminated by the residual light of his fire spells, ready to continue the confrontation, but hoping that the dragon would finally listen to reason.

"The Firm One" , defiant to the end, continued his assault on Kaen, launching attacks with a ferocity that shook the very core of the kingdom of fire. Each onslaught, charged with the full extent of his ancient power, was destined to crush any resistance that stood against him. However, Kaen, with supernatural ability, repelled each blow with an ease that defied the comprehension of everyone present.

The air was charged with palpable tension as "The Firm One" in an act of overwhelming frustration, raised his voice in a roar that reverberated through the palace walls and beyond. "The Wild One", show your face! Stop hiding behind your subordinate!" he demanded, his voice a mix of anger and desperation, imploring the fire dragon to intervene directly in the conflict.

Despite the earth dragon's powerful calls, there was no response from the legendary "The Wild One". Kaen, in the midst of the chaos, maintained his imperturbable posture, his every movement a testament to the absolute mastery he exerted over the fire. The fight, though one-sided in its execution, resonated throughout the kingdom and beyond, sending shockwaves across the world, reaching even the most remote corners.

Exhausted by the futility of his efforts and lack of progress, Kaen made a bold decision. With a dramatic gesture, he raised both hands, summoning a fiery tornado of epic proportions. The flames coiled around them both, forming a prison of fire that imprisoned Kaen and "The Firm One" together.

Within this fiery vortex, the air was filled with heat and the noise of fire. Kaen, now face to face with the earth dragon in a confined space of his own creation, began to speak. His voice, although calm, carried a weight of sincerity and urgency that completely captured "The Firm One's" attention.

"Listen, before you judge," Kaen began, his gaze fixed on the dragon's eyes. "The history you know and the reality you perceive may not be all it seems. There are truths hidden in the shadows of power and legacies that extend beyond our current understanding."

As "The Firm One" listened, captive within the fiery tornado, Kaen was about to reveal crucial details of his past and the true nature of his power, promising to unravel the mysteries that had led to so much conflict and despair. The promise of these revelations and the forced intimacy of confinement promised to change the course of their confrontation and, possibly, the fate of all the kingdoms involved.

Kaen, locked in the fiery vortex with "The Firm One" began to tell his story, his calm but firm voice echoing above the crackling of the flames. His story not only sought to inform the earth dragon, but also to clarify the truths hidden behind its unusual power and position.

"My life began humble and lonely," Kaen began, his gaze lost in memories of the past. "I was born in a small, isolated village in the vast lands of the kingdom of fire, raised by a community that respected the power of fire, but also feared its destructive potential."

Kaen described his childhood as that of an orphaned boy, adopted by the town after being found near one of the many active volcanic craters that dot the landscape of the kingdom of fire. From very early on, Kaen displayed an unusual affinity with fire, a talent that distinguished him among his peers and also marked him as an outsider.

"As I grew older," Kaen continued, "my connection to fire deepened. It wasn't just skill or training; it was something more primal, a voice that resonated within me, guiding me, teaching me." Kaen revealed how, during his lonely nights, he heard what he believed to be the whisper of the Fire Dragon, "The Wild One", speaking to him through the flames, telling him ancient secrets of the world and the element he mastered.

"These encounters transformed me," he explained. "I became more than a mere manipulator of fire; I became its living embodiment, able to feel its pulse, anticipate its flow, and control its outbursts with mere will."

His adolescence was a period of self-imposed isolation, dedicated to perfecting his mastery over fire under the invisible tutelage of "The Wild One". Kaen trained in the deserts and volcanic mountains, forging his body and spirit in the furnace of nature's most brutal.

"When the time came for the Fire Tournament," Kaen said, changing his tone to one of nostalgia mixed with pride, "I was ready. My skill was such that no other competitor could match me, not by sheer strength, but by my understanding of the fire as an extension of my own being."

After winning the tournament and being proclaimed sovereign, Kaen had not only achieved legendary status among his people, but had also solidified his connection with "The Wild One", who had entrusted him with secrets and powers that went beyond any human expectation.

As "The Firm One" listened, visibly absorbed by the story, Kaen prepared to reveal the biggest secret of all: the true nature of his relationship with "The Wild One" and how this had influenced not only his life, but destiny. of the entire kingdom of fire.

At the heart of the fiery vortex, as flames danced around them, creating a barrier between them and the outside world, Kaen recounted the peak of their journey, the defining moment of their transformation and ascent.

"The night before the final of the Fire Tournament, I was summoned to a secret place in the heart of the volcanic mountains, an ancient sanctuary known only to a few," Kaen began, his voice taking on an almost reverent tone as he recalled that encounter. crucial. "There, in the midst of rivers of lava and columns of fire, "The Wild One" appeared to me in all his fiery majesty."

The air around them seemed to vibrate with the intensity of their story. Kaen described how the dragon, a towering creature with scales that glowed like burning coals and eyes that burned with the power of the sun itself, descended before him not as a conqueror, but as a mentor and guide.

""The Wild One" spoke to me not only with words, but with visions of fire, showing me the web of connections that linked all the elements, and how fire was the heart that drove change and renewal," Kaen explained. "He revealed to me that he had been watching over me since I was a child, guiding me toward this destiny."

The most shocking revelation came later, when "The Wild One" expressed his intention to leave this world, not through death, but through a transformation. "He decided that it was time for his essence to pass into a new form, that the world no longer needed dragons as direct guardians, but should be led by those who lived and breathed within its confines," Kaen said, the flames reflecting a spectrum of emotions on his face.

"At the peak of the volcano, in an ancient ritual that resonated with echoes of a time when the earth was young, "The Wild One" began the transfer of his power. It was a fiery process, where every flame that touched my skin did not burn, but he instilled in me a strength and knowledge beyond the human. And so, without dying, ""The Wild One" dissolved into the air, leaving me not only as his heir but as his reincarnation."

Kaen paused, letting "The Firm One" absorb the magnitude of what that revelation meant. "Since that day, I have carried within me not only the power of a dragon, but the responsibility of maintaining the balance that "The Wild One" had protected for millennia."

"The Firm One" looks at Kaen, not just as a human or a sovereign, but as the new manifestation of an entity he once revered as the leader and protector of his element. The atmosphere was charged with a mix of awe, disbelief, and new understanding, as the flames of the fire tornado continued to roar, symbolizing not only the power of Kaen, but also the fiery legacy of "The Wild One" that now lived through him.

The air grew thick and hot as "The Firm One" vehemently rejected Kaen's story. "Impossible!" roared the dragon, its voice echoing in the confines of the fiery tornado. "The Wild One" would never abandon his essence to a mortal, much less dissolve his existence into such a fragile form!"

Enraged and confused, "The Firm One" launched another attack, this time with renewed ferocity, as if attempting to deny the reality of Kaen's words with the sheer force of his earthly power. Rocks and debris flew toward Kaen with devastating speed, each imbued with the telluric energy of the earth dragon.

However, Kaen remained unfazed. With absolute calm, he raised his hands, and an aura of intense flames surrounded his body, disintegrating the projectiles before they could touch him. "You do not wish to believe because you fear the truth of a changing world," Kaen said, his voice as firm and powerful as the very fire he commanded.

"The Firm One", still unwilling to give in, launched one last offensive, a gigantic wave of earth and stone that rushed like a tsunami towards Kaen. With a determined gesture, Kaen conjured a blast of fire so intense and concentrated that the wave instantly vaporized, leaving behind only a trail of steam and ash.

Seeing that "The Firm One" was about to launch another attack, Kaen accelerated the end of his demonstration. With surprising speed, he closed the distance between them and, in one fluid motion, climbed onto the enormous dragon's back. Placing a hand on the dragon's head and pointing his weapon just behind its skull, Kaen said clearly, "Understand, I seek not your end, but your understanding and acceptance that the world is no longer as it was."

"The Firm One" stopped, his body still vibrating with the energy of the battle. The tension was palpable in the hot air, but the dragon, overwhelmed and subjugated by Kaen's immense power, finally lowered its head in a gesture of temporary submission. "Explain to me then," he growled with relative resignation, "if what you say is true, what is the purpose of all this?"

Kaen watches from his dominant position, not only physically but also morally, over the earth dragon. "Our fight must be for something greater than ourselves," Kaen responded, preparing to deliver a final lesson that could change not only the outlook of "The Firm One" but also the future of all kingdoms.

As the flames of the fire tornado began to subside, the hot air was filled with an expectant tension. Kaen, still standing over "The Firm One" , felt the dragon's resistance give way under the revelation of the truth and the recognition of the essence of "The Wild One".

"We may not fully understand the motives of those who guide us," Kaen said, his voice soft but firm, "but we can choose what to do with the legacy they leave us. I have chosen to honor "The Wild One" not only with words, but with actions that seek the peace and prosperity of all our kingdoms."

The earth dragon, whose fury had been so ferocious and destructive, was now visibly calming down. He closed his huge eyes, concentrating on the energy flowing from Kaen. As he did so, the scales covering his body seemed to glow slightly, reflecting not only the physical fire that surrounded them, but also the internal change he was undergoing.

Opening his eyes, "The Firm One" looked at Kaen with a new light of understanding. "I feel... I feel the presence of "The Wild One" in you," he admitted with a soft growl, his tone filled with wonder and a new reverence. "It's a part of you now, as clearly as the mountains are a part of my essence."

Kaen nodded, stepping down from the dominant position, but maintaining a cautious respect for the powerful creature before him. "And just as the mountains stand firm and solid, so must our resolve to maintain peace and stability. We owe that to ourselves and to future generations."

With one last glance at the now restored fire palace in the distance, "The Firm One" nodded slowly. "I will return to my kingdom," he announced, "to meditate on these revelations and readjust my path. Perhaps the time has come for the dragons, too, to change our way of guarding this world."

Without another word, the earth dragon spread its great wings and, with a mighty beat, rose into the sky, leaving a trail of dust and a promise of reflection and possible change. Kaen watched their departure, feeling a weight of responsibility and hope in his heart.

Kaen returned once again inside his palace, ready to continue his rule not only as ruler of fire, but as guardian of a legacy that now transcended generations and species. The fighting was over, at least for now, but the path to true peace and understanding was just beginning.

Chapter X: Echoes of a Silenced Past

Fen, with a heavy heart and a mind full of unanswered questions, was heading back towards the crater where it had all started. The memories of that fateful day, when the meteor had burst into his life, taking everything he loved, still burned inside him like an unquenchable fire. His step was firm, each movement driven by the determination to unlock hidden secrets and gain the power needed to protect what he still had left.

Arriving at the crater, Fen expected to find some vestige of ancient magic or traces of the cosmic conflict he had felt the last time he was there. However, to his surprise and dismay, the area was immaculate, as if the land itself had been cleansed of any trace of magic or disaster. There was no sign of the meteor, nor the devastation it had caused. It was as if someone had deliberately erased all traces of what had happened.

Fen knelt, running his hands over the cold, soft earth, searching for any signs that might have been overlooked. But there was nothing, only the silence and solitude of a place that had once been an epicenter of power and tragedy. The lack of evidence left him with more questions than answers, fueling frustration and anguish in his heart.

His mind churning with confusion, Fen sat on the edge of the crater, staring out into the void that now seemed so ordinary. He reflected on his journey, on the battles fought and the losses suffered. Despite his efforts and sacrifices, he seemed to be no closer to the truth than he was at the beginning. The desolation of that thought enveloped him like a cold fog.

"It can't be in vain," he murmured to himself, the wind carrying his words as if they were part of nature's whisper. The silence of the place offered little comfort, and the lack of answers only served to fan the flame of his determination. Fen knew he couldn't afford to give up, not while the mystery of his family's death remained unsolved and the threat of an unknown power continued to lurk in the shadows.

As twilight fell, Fen rose, his figure silhouetted against the dying sky that painted the horizon in shades of purple and gold. It was time to return to the only place that might have the answers he needed, the place where he had lost everything and where perhaps he could find the key to preventing others from suffering as he had suffered.

Looking once more towards the crater, now calm and deceptively peaceful, Fen turned around and began his descent. Each step took him physically away from that emptiness, but brought him closer to the inevitable confrontation with his past and, perhaps, to the definitive confrontation with those who had unleashed the chain of events that had marked his destiny.

As Fen leaves the summit behind, the image of his solitary silhouette blending with the shadows that lengthened the night, a man searching for justice in a world that seemed determined to hide its darkest secrets.

Fen walked with purposeful steps toward his old home, the place where it all began and where he had lost so much. With every step he took towards the village, memories of happy days intermingled with images of the tragedy that had erased that happiness. He was almost within reach of his goal, his mind focused on what he hoped to find or rediscover in the ashes of his past.

However, just as the familiar silhouette of his village began to appear on the horizon at dusk, an imposing and unexpected presence materialized before him, stopping his progress. It was "The Pacific", the Water Dragon, whose appearance was as surprising as the place and time of their meeting.

The figure of the dragon stood majestically, imposing and serene, cutting the distance between heaven and earth. Its scales shone with the reflection of the water under the last rays of the sun, and it's deep eyes seemed to contain the vastness of the ocean. Fen stopped, his heart pounding under the dragon's piercing gaze.

"The Pacific" watched him silently for a moment, as if assessing Fen's very essence before speaking. The atmosphere was charged with a mixture of awe and slight tension, as the wind carried the soft murmur of leaves and the distant crash of waves, remembering the influence of the dragon on its element.

Fen, although initially surprised and cautious, maintained his composure. He did not draw his sword, understanding that the dragon's presence did not herald combat, but something deeper and more significant. He took a deep breath, preparing to listen and respond, knowing that the words they would exchange could have immense weight on his path already fraught with searches and revelations.

The presence of the Water Dragon at this critical point, just before Fen could reenter the remains of his past, marked a moment of pause, an invitation to reflect deeply before continuing. With both facing each other, the warrior and the dragon, under the twilight that dyed the sky in tones of fire and water, symbolizing the convergence of their paths and the beginning of a conversation that could change the course of history.

In the stillness before dusk, Fen and "The Pacific" stood face to face, the tension of the moment intertwined with the soft breeze that carried the smell of damp earth and sea salt. The warrior listened, his expression a mixture of surprise and caution, as the dragon began to reveal the recent events and their profound implications.

""The Changeling" and I have watched with growing concern the developments in the realm of fire," "The Pacific" began, his voice echoing with the depth of calm oceans. "The energy emanating from that place has begun to upset the delicate balance we have maintained for millennia. It is not just a question of power, but of harmony between all the elements that make up our world."

Fen, whose face reflected the seriousness of the situation, nodded slowly. He remembered the subtle but noticeable changes in the environment as he approached his home, a silent confirmation of the dragon's words.

""The Changeling" and I have decided that it is time to act directly," the dragon continued. "The eras when dragons stood aside have passed. If ancient wars are to be avoided and peace preserved, we must intervene before the current imbalances deepen."

The mention of the ancient wars sent a shiver down Fen's spine. The history of their world was marked by catastrophic conflicts that had reshaped continents and kingdoms, leaving scars that had barely begun to heal.

"And what is expected of me in all this?" Fen asked, his voice heavy with a mix of honor and weight. He knew that his personal journey for justice was intertwined with these greater responsibilities, but he needed to understand his exact role in the dragons' plan.

""The Changeling" and I wish you to be our link, our champion," "The Pacific" explained. "With your unique connection to water, and your experience in dealing with the challenges of the human realms, you are the ideal candidate to help us mediate and, if necessary, intervene directly."

Fen stood thoughtfully, the magnitude of the task before him as vast as the ocean itself. It wasn't just a quest for revenge or personal redemption; It was a call to serve as a pillar in the defense of global balance.

"I understand," Fen finally said, looking up to meet the dragon's eyes, where the reflection of twilight played in the watery depths. "I will do whatever it takes to help. My journey, my fight, has not been about me alone for a long time."

"The Pacific" nodded, a wave of relief and hope seeming to flow from his being. "Then prepare yourself, Fen. What lies ahead will be a test not only of your strength and skill, but also of your heart and your will."

The warrior and the dragon, looking to the west, where the last rays of the sun were sinking into the horizon, promising both the end of a day and the dawn of a new era of intervention and unity between the kingdoms. Fen felt empowered, not only by the power of the water flowing through him, but also by the new purpose he had agreed to embrace.

Under the twilight that painted the sky with reddish and blue hues, Fen and "The Pacific" continued their dialogue on the seashore, the waves whispering promises and warnings with each break. Fen, with his gaze fixed on the horizon, shared his vision, not of ambition for power, but of the search for justice and peace.

"I do not aspire to crowns or thrones," Fen stated, his voice firm despite the sea wind that played with his hair. "My fight is against the pain and destruction that has spread like a disease across our kingdoms. If my sacrifice can prevent another child from losing their home, or another family from being torn apart, then it will be a sacrifice I will make without hesitation."

The Water Dragon, "The Pacific", watched Fen's resolution with a mixture of admiration and reflection. The warrior's sincerity and his reluctance to seek power for power's sake struck a deep chord in the dragon's ancient soul. In the world of dragons, where power and strength were often the currency of exchange, finding such a pure heart was both a rarity and a reminder of what was at stake.

Fen's words, charged with a burning desire for justice and reparation, prompted "The Pacific" to reconsider his own perception of the warrior's destiny. "Your words and your spirit are a testament to the strength that comes not from domination, but from sacrifice and compassion," the dragon said, his voice a soft murmur over the sound of the waves.

The dragon took a few steps towards the water, looking into the depths that reflected the rising stars. "Your vision for the future, your reluctance to lead out of desire for power, makes the decision I am about to make one of the most significant in my long life," he continued, his eyes twinkling with a gleam of determination and excitement.

Fen watched, expectant and slightly anxious, as "The Pacific" seemed to sink into a deep state of contemplation. The air around them vibrated with the energy of impending decisions, changes that could alter not only their own destinies, but also the balance of the entire world.

With "The Pacific" turning to Fen, a clear decision in his eyes. "I am about to take an action that will change our world, Fen. An action inspired by your strength and your sacrifice," the dragon announced, setting the stage for revelations and decisions that would resonate across the realms.

Before the serene shore of the kingdom of water, "The Pacific" contemplated Fen with a deep and ancestral gaze. His decision to merge his essence with a human was not an impulsive act, but the result of centuries of accumulated wisdom and a deep understanding of the changing times.

"What we are about to do," "The Pacific" began, his voice echoing with the murmur of the waves, "requires an act of magic that is unprecedented in our history. It is not simply sharing power, but intertwining our souls." so that they coexist in harmony."

Fen listened, his heart beating with the tides, aware of the weight of his next step. "How is such a union possible?" he asked with reverence and curiosity.

"The Pacific" raised one of its powerful claws, revealing the intricate dark blue patterns that glowed on its scaly skin. "Over the millennia, I have studied the hidden currents of the world, the lines that connect life and the elements. I have discovered that, at the core of every being, there is a point of possible convergence, a place where two essences can meet and merge without destroying each other."

"This magic," the dragon continued, "I have forged from the bottom of the ocean, from the pearls of the depths that have absorbed the wisdom of the water for ages. With them, I have created a spell that will allow us to unite our forces in a way that respects our individuality but amplifies our power."

Fen nodded, understanding the magnitude of the commitment. "And what will the process be like?"

"The Pacific" explained that the fusion would be a delicate ritual, which would require Fen to completely surrender his being, a complete openness to the tides of destiny. "I will place these pearls in a circle around us, and each one will radiate a fragment of my essence. As we recite the song of the depths, the pearls will activate the spell and our souls will begin to intertwine."

"You will feel a surge of power, like a high tide filling every corner of your being. Don't resist; let yourself be carried away by the current. It is vital that you keep your heart open and your mind clear, because during this process, you will be both the anchor and the sailboat on our shared trip."

Fen took a deep breath, his resolve reinforced by the solemnity of the moment. "I'm ready," he said, his voice no more than a whisper, but firm as the seabed.

"The Pacific" nodded, and with a majestic gesture, began to place the mystical pearls around them, each one humming with the power of the ocean. As the circle closed, the pearls began to glow, bathing the shore in a blue and green light that seemed to emanate directly from the heart of the sea.

Now with both dragon and human standing within the circle of pearls, the air vibrant with the promise of what was to come. "The Pacific" began to recite the ancient song of the depths, his voice an echo of the underwater world, and Fen, closing his eyes, prepared to cross the threshold towards an unknown destiny, but inevitably intertwined with that of his new companion.

The night sky lit up with a flash that rivaled the brilliance of the stars. The light emanated from the ritual between Fen and "The Pacific" was so powerful and dazzling that its energy echoed throughout all the realms. Throughout the land, the inhabitants looked up at the sky, amazed and confused, without understanding the origin or meaning of that phenomenon.

In the water kingdom, the ritual had reached its climax. The mystical pearls that "The Pacific" had arranged around them shone with supernatural intensity, forming a vortex of water and light that enveloped Fen. As the dragon's song filled the air, waves of water power intertwined with Fen's human essence, weaving a new existence.

Fen felt his body and spirit becoming saturated with immense energy. The Water Dragon's presence fused with his own, uniting his ancient wisdom and elemental mastery with Fen's determination and human bravery. This process, far from being painful, was a revelation, an awakening to a world that I now perceived with astonishing clarity and depth.

With the conclusion of the ritual, the light began to gradually dissipate, leaving Fen transformed on the edge of the water realm. His eyes, now a deep blue hue that reflected the depths of the ocean, looked at the world with a new perspective. His body radiated a soft bluish glow, a constant reminder of the presence and power of "The Pacific" within him.

"You are now more than human, more than dragon," "The Pacific" murmured through Fen's voice, his tone filled with pride and hope. "You are the guardian of our combined wills, the protector of the balance that must prevail."

With his new form and the power of water coursing through his veins, Fen felt more prepared than ever to continue his journey.

Not only did he seek justice for his past, but he now also carried the responsibility of protecting the balance of the world, a burden he accepted with honor and determination.

Fen leaving the shore, his lone figure silhouetted against the full moon. Every step he took towards his next destination was guided by a stronger conviction and a power that he felt to the depths of his being. It was the beginning of a new phase in his adventure, armed with the power of a dragon and the heart of a human, ready to face any challenge that might arise on his path to truth and harmony.

In the depths of twilight, Fen headed towards the realm of fire, with the essence of the Water Dragon flowing within him. "The Pacific" had urged him to look for answers in that place, suggesting that the heart of the conflict and the key to peace lay there.

Simultaneously, in the different corners of the world, every guardian dragon of the remaining kingdoms felt the resonance of the changes that were taking place. "The Firm One" of the earth realm, "The Changeling" of the air, and the other guardians were contemplating the course of their future actions. The vibrations of the ritual between Fen and "The Pacific" had reached each of them, sparking deep reflection on their role in the times to come.

In the kingdom of fire, unrest grew. Rumors of a human transformed into something more than a mere mortal spread like wildfire among the population and court of Kaen. The king, aware of the powers that he himself wielded after his encounter with "The Wild One", prepared for the inevitable. He knew that Fen's arrival could mean a monumental change for his kingdom and possibly all kingdoms.

Meanwhile, in the realms of water, earth, and air, the guardian dragons were beginning to mobilize. "The Firm One" considered leaving his isolation to intervene directly, given the magnitude of the energy displayed in the fusion ritual. "The Changeling", always the most elusive, sent his own emissaries to gather information, while he meditated on the wind and its implications.

Fen's journey to the kingdom of fire was full of omens. The sky above him was dyed with shades of red and orange, reflecting the internal flames that were now part of his being. With each step, his determination grew stronger, driven by the certainty that he was on the right path.

"The answers you seek will not be revealed easily," "The Pacific" had warned him. "But the truth always finds a way to emerge, especially when guided by justice and balance."

With the world possibly on the brink of a new era, Fen moved forward, aware of the weight of his new responsibility. He carried with him not only the power of a dragon, but also the fate of many, woven into the tapestry of his decisions. The battle for the truth would not be his alone; It would be a struggle shared with the ancient guardians of the world, each evaluating the extent to which they should intervene in the affairs of mortals.

As Fen reaches the borders of the kingdom of fire, the silhouette of the volcanic peaks silhouetted against the twilight sky. The earth beneath his feet vibrates slightly, an echo of the power he now carries within, ready to face whatever it takes to restore balance and uncover the truth hidden beneath layers of mystery and time.

Chapter XI: Shadows and Fire

Fen, with the essence of the Water Dragon still pulsating in his being, found himself again in front of Kaen, in the heart of the kingdom of fire. The palace, rebuilt and resplendent under a red-tinted sky, seemed to reflect the tension in the air.

"Kaen, I need answers," Fen said with a firm voice, reflecting the new strength within him. "And I need to talk to "The Wild One". I believe there are truths between our kingdoms that have not yet come to light."

Kaen, with an expression that mixed serenity with caution, shook his head slowly. "Fen, I have tried to explain to you before. There is no such alliance between our kingdom and that of the earth, and... "The Wild One" is no longer in this world. I cannot grant you an audience that is impossible."

Kaen's words fell on Fen like a heavy curtain of disbelief. The water warrior struggled to process this new information, his mind torn between disappointment and suspicion.

"You must go, Fen. There is nothing here for you, and your presence only portends conflicts I would rather avoid," Kaen continued, extending a hand in a pacifying but firm gesture.

While the two were talking, on the outskirts of the kingdom, a different tension was brewing. "The Changeling" and "The Firm One" watched from a distance, their powerful forms barely visible among the shadows and steam emanating from the earth. They knew that their intervention could be imminent, depending on the outcome of the conversation in the palace.

"The Firm One", with his body covered in dirt and stone, growled softly, restless and ready to act if the situation required it.

Meanwhile, "The Changeling", ever enigmatic, floated in the air, his thoughts as unpredictable as the wind around him.

The meeting between Fen and Kaen did not appear to be heading towards a peaceful resolution. Fen, despite his new power and wisdom, felt growing frustration. He was not willing to leave the kingdom of fire without the answers he had come to seek.

Just as the conversation reached a critical point, a subtle but noticeable gust of cold wind and earth vibration signaled the growing impatience of the outer dragons. Kaen sensed these signs, and a shadow of worry crossed his face, aware that the powers stirring beyond his walls might not be so easily appeased.

Fen stood immovable in front of Kaen, while in the shadows, the dragons prepared for what they knew could be an inevitable confrontation. The fate of Fen, Kaen, and possibly all the kingdoms hung in a delicate balance, awaiting a spark that could kindle the flames of conflict or light the path to new understanding.

Fen, tired of waiting, launched an attack against Kaen as a warning, showing that he was not afraid to face each other once again although that was not his wish. Given this, Kaen also launched a warning attack at Fen but he repelled it without any problems.

Kaen, visibly impressed by Fen's enhanced skill, understood that a direct confrontation in the heart of the fire kingdom would only bring more devastation, something he wished to avoid at all costs. With a sigh of resignation, he accepted Fen's determination and proposed a change of scenery for their duel.

"If you truly wish to confront me to get your answers," Kaen said seriously, "then let us do so away from the innocent. I do not wish to see any more destruction in the lands I swore to protect."

Fen, although surprised by Kaen's offer, understood the wisdom of avoiding unnecessary harm to the citizens of the fire kingdom.

He nodded determinedly, willing to follow Kaen to a more secluded location where their conflict could be resolved without putting others at risk.

Both warriors walked in silence towards the outskirts of the kingdom, each step echoing with the tension of what was to come. Upon reaching a vast desolate plain, surrounded by the volcanic mountains that marked the limit of the kingdom of fire, they stopped. The place was ideal for a duel of such magnitude: far from any settlement and surrounded by untamed nature that could absorb and reflect the intensity of their confrontation.

As they prepared to begin, "The Changeling" and "The Firm One" watched from above, ready to intervene if the situation required it. The air was charged with electricity, a mixture of anticipation and fear for the possible consequences of this confrontation.

Kaen and Fen stood facing each other, the heat of the surroundings and the cold wind around them creating a palpable contrast. With one last look of mutual understanding, they both knew that what followed could change not only their own destinies, but the course of the entire world.

Now with both warriors throwing their powers against each other, beginning a combat that would echo through the kingdoms, an epic showdown where fire and water not only fought for dominance, but also to discover the hidden truth behind the secrets. long kept.

The air was tense and vibrant with energy as Fen and Kaen faced off on the outskirts of the fire kingdom. With each move, they demonstrated exceptional mastery over their respective elements, in a duel that seemed as old as time itself.

Fen, fused with the power of the Water Dragon, manipulated the liquid with impressive grace and precision. Their attacks consisted of gigantic waves and jets of pressurized water that were launched towards Kaen with the force of a tsunami. Each blow of water carried with it the cold of the ocean, trying to extinguish the flames of its adversary.

For his part, Kaen, who housed the essence of "The Wild One", controlled fire with a burning intensity. His counterattacks were flames and columns of fire that rose from the ground, seeking to consume the water and overcome the cold barrier that Fen erected. The earth around them charred under the extreme heat, and the air filled with steam every time their fires met water.

The clash of fire and water was not only spectacular to look at, but also generated a symphony of sounds that echoed through the realm of fire and beyond. Explosions of steam upon contact with the elements rumbled like thunder, while the hiss of evaporating water and crackling flames created a constant chorus that warned everyone of the magnitude of the confrontation.

As the battle dragged on, neither Fen nor Kaen showed any signs of fatigue. The energy of the dragons within them sustained them, allowing them to continue with an intensity that did not diminish. The attacks followed one after another, in an endless cycle of assaults and counterattacks that demonstrated parity in their power and skill.

The fight continued for hours, under the watchful eye of "The Changeling" and "The Firm One" from above. Although prepared to intervene, the dragons watched with growing respect and awe as these two warriors fought with a ferocity that rivaled that of the mythical beings themselves.

With each exchange, the combat was felt throughout the kingdom. The vibrations of their fight altered the earth and air, causing the citizens of the kingdom of fire to feel the resonance of the battle in their homes and hearts. The parity between the combatants was such that, despite the hours that had passed, none showed a clear advantage, each one adapting and responding with a power that seemed inexhaustible.

Thus, with the sky tinted by the glow of combat and the earth trembling beneath them, Fen and Kaen continued their epic battle, a duel that seemed destined to define the future of their world.

As the battle between Fen and Kaen reached an unprecedented level of intensity, their overflowing power seemed to threaten the very stability of the world. Just as both warriors were launching into a clash that promised to be catastrophic, the air and the earth trembled with the sudden appearance of "The Changeling" and "The Firm One".

The silence that followed was profound, almost unearthly, as the combatants and spectators stood still, overwhelmed by the majesty and power of the two dragons. The presence of these mythical creatures enveloped the battlefield in a tense calm, a respite from the storm of fire and water.

"The Changeling", elegant and serene, floated near Fen, its wings generating gentle currents of air that seemed to whisper words of wisdom and support. He looked at Fen with a depth that went beyond mere perception, recognizing in him a spirit kindred to his own desire for balance and truth. With a subtle but powerful gesture, he strengthened Fen's aura, increasing the intensity and range of his water attacks.

For his part, "The Firm One" posed with an imposing solidity next to Kaen, his presence like an unbreakable mountain. The earth beneath his feet seemed to solidify even more, and with a low growl, he instilled in Kaen a resistance that redoubled his vigor and strength. Their support not only strengthened Kaen's defense, but also gave him renewed power, allowing him to meet Fen's onslaught with unwavering determination.

The battle resumed with these new allies at their side, but now there was a different balance. Fen, supported by the agility and air strategy that "The Changeling" provided him, moved with a grace that contrasted with the brute strength that "The Firm One" gave Kaen. The clash of their powers was not only a fight between two warriors, but a manifestation of the eternal battle between the elements themselves.

The attacks occurred with a speed and ferocity that reflected the passion and urgency of both sides. Each blow resonated through the kingdom, sending vibrations that were felt by all inhabitants, a constant reminder of the epic combat that would decide the future of their world.

With each passing minute, the fight between Fen and Kaen, now amplified and modulated by the presence of the dragons, became more than just a duel; It was a symbol of changing times and the fight for the right to decide the fate of the world. As the sun began to decline on the horizon, the battle showed no signs of ending, each combatant matching and countering the other's powers in a spectacle of strength, will, and indomitable heart.

In a haven of calm during the storm of battle, Fen's mind was transported to a recent encounter that had been crucial in "The Changeling's" decision to support his cause. The memory unfolded like a vision before his eyes, taking him back to the moment when "The Changeling" had conversed with "The Pacific".

At that meeting, "The Changeling" had listened carefully to the concerns of "The Pacific" about the challenges facing the world. The water dragon had shared his deep connection with Fen, his decision to merge with him, and his belief in the need for a new order where humans played a central role in protecting the balance of the world. The sincerity and passion with which "The Pacific" spoke of Fen and his ideals had resonated deeply with

"The Changeling", awakening an empathy that had been dormant for eons. Moved by these revelations, "The Changeling" had decided that supporting Fen was supporting the evolution of the world towards a future in which dragons were not direct guardians, but mentors from the shadows.

On the other hand, "The Firm One" had reached a similar conclusion, but through a more introspective and solitary process. After his confrontation with Kaen, where he had perceived the strength and determination of the young ruler, "The Firm One" had retreated to the depths of the Earth's mountains to meditate. For days, he had reflected on the history of the world, the evolution of humans, and his own role as guardian of the earth element.

"The Firm One"remembered clearly the moment when, beneath the heavy mantle of the earth, he had felt a subtle but powerful change in the fabric of the world. This change had led him to the realization that times were, in fact, changing, and that perhaps it was time to allow humans to take the reins of their own destiny. The decision to support Kaen had been an act of faith in the potential of humans to grow and take on greater responsibilities.

These memories and revelations filled Fen with renewed determination as he returned to the present, just in time to stop a new assault from Kaen. With every move and every decision made on the battlefield, Fen not only fought for his personal cause, but also represented the new path that "The Pacific" and "The Changeling" saw for the world, a future where balance would be maintained. not only because of the strength of the dragons, but because of the wisdom and courage of humans.

As the sun fell and rose countless times, the battle between Fen and Kaen raged on with no signs of ending. Days, or perhaps weeks, might have passed as the combatants, driven by forces beyond their understanding, continued to engage in an unprecedented duel. Fatigue and wear and tear were evident in every movement, but Fen especially was showing signs of extreme exhaustion that went beyond the physical.

Fen's transformation was gradual but alarming. Initially moved by a noble cause, his fight began to deteriorate as fatigue undermined his mental resistance. His face, once marked by determination, now reflected uncontrolled ferocity. The power of the water, combined with his repressed pain and fury, began to manifest in a more violent and chaotic form.

On the battlefield, Fen became a living storm. Every blow he threw was infused with renewed rage, fueled by memories of the loss and pain that the supposed alliance between the realms of fire and earth had caused in his life. His attacks no longer had the precision or control they had before; They were brutal, unbridled, reflecting the internal storm that consumed him.

Kaen, watching from a distance as he dodged and countered each assault, noticed the change in Fen. Although concerned about the downward spiral Fen seemed to be trapped in, he also recognized a critical opportunity to end the conflict. With the serenity that characterized him, Kaen calculated his final move, preparing to take advantage of Fen's lack of control to launch a decisive attack.

Just before the final clash, the battlefield fell into a foreboding silence. The wind ceased, and the flames surrounding the area seemed to hold their breath. Kaen, determination clear in his eyes, surged forward, channeling all of his energy into a single, devastating blow aimed at Fen.

Fen, lost in his fury, barely registered Kaen's approach. His mind was clouded by images of his lost family and destroyed home, driving him to fight with an almost supernatural ferocity. At that critical moment, the warrior no longer seemed human; He was the very embodiment of revenge and pain, a specter of war that knew no limits or fear.

Now with Kaen speeding towards Fen, the impending impact promised to be devastating. The tension is palpable, each second stretching as if time itself awaits the outcome of this titanic showdown. The question of what will happen when the unstoppable force of Kaen collides with the uncontrollable Fen is left hanging in the air.

From above, "The Changeling" and "The Firm One" faced each other in a fight that seemed to mirror the chaos that was unfolding on the ground. Both dragons, each supporting their respective champion, unleashed forces that shook the sky and the earth, each trying to gain an advantage over the other to influence the outcome of the duel between Fen and Kaen.

"The Firm One" used his control over the land to launch masses of rocks and create earth barriers that attempted to block or deflect "The Changeling's" air attacks. On the other hand, "The Changeling", with the agility and speed that characterizes the wind, dodged and counterattacked, sending gusts of cutting air that split the rocks and altered the land formations created by his opponent.

As Kaen launched his final attack towards Fen, "The Changeling" saw an opportunity to intervene. With a quick and precise maneuver, he slipped through the defense of "The Firm One", who was momentarily distracted by a particularly powerful counterattack from Kaen. "The Changeling" rushed towards the battlefield, just as Kaen approached Fen.

In a flash of light and wind, "The Changeling" intercepted Kaen, deflecting his killing blow. However, in that moment of confusion and relief, Fen, still consumed by his berserker state, reacted with unexpected ferocity. He leapt toward "The Changeling", mounting his head with surprising agility. Fury and pain had blinded Fen to the point of not recognizing his ally.

Fen, moved by a dark, primal instinct, extended his hand, now engulfed in a vortex of water that spun with voracious energy. With a scream that resonated with the entire storm of emotions that consumed him, he slammed his hand into "The Changeling's" head. The contact was electric and devastating. Dragon energy began to flow into Fen, a torrent of power and ancient wisdom pouring into the human warrior.

"The Changeling", taken by surprise and unable to defend himself, felt his essence being quickly absorbed. The transfer of power was intense and abrupt, leaving the dragon in a state of critical weakness. Around them, heaven and earth seemed to rumble in response to Fen's desperate and destructive act.

In that dramatic climax, with Fen still on "The Changeling's" head, absorbing his essence. The uncertainty about the consequences of this act and the final state of both, Fen and

"The Changeling", keeps all witnesses of this epic battle in suspense. What future awaits Fen now that he has taken on the power of a dragon? And what will become of "The Changeling", weakened and possibly on the verge of disappearance?

The visual and emotional impact of Fen's final act reverberated across the vast desolate plain, affecting everyone, but especially Kaen and "The Firm One" As Fen consumed the essence of "The Changeling", the dragon's body began to fade, its glowing outlines dissolving into the air, until nothing remained, only the echo of its power now flowing through Fen.

Kaen, his expression marked by horror and disbelief, stepped back instinctively. He had never witnessed or imagined that a human could completely absorb a dragon, a being of such magnitude and power. The image of Fen, with her body enveloped in a torrential current of energy that gave her an almost divine aura, left him speechless. The intensity of the moment was reflected in his eyes, which went from shock to fear, realizing that Fen's power had reached a level that might not be possible to contain or combat.

"The Firm One", for his part, roared with a mixture of anger and grief. The loss of "The Changeling" was not just an unexpected blow between allies, but a profound disturbance in the balance of elemental powers. Despite his own strength as a dragon, Fen's act highlighted a critical vulnerability in his existence. The earth dragon, its scales trembling with suppressed fury, looked at Fen with a new respect mixed with deep wariness.

The silence was broken by the sound of earth and fire colliding in the background, a constant reminder of the tumult that still throbbed beneath the calm surface of the confrontation. Kaen, regaining his composure, knew he had to act prudently. Despite his initial desire to end the fight, he now had to reconsider his strategy to not only confront Fen, but to ensure the survival of his own kingdom and perhaps all kingdoms.

Meanwhile, Fen, now imbued with the power of "The Changeling", seemed more composed but infinitely more dangerous. The fury had left his face, replaced by an unearthly calm. His eyes, once burning with rage, now glowed with a cold understanding of the new capabilities he possessed.

On the outskirts of the battlefield, the spectators, both mortals and those from other realms who had sensed what had happened, murmured among themselves, whispering about the meaning of this new development. The question on everyone's mind was clear: What did this mean for the future of their world? How could there be balance and peace with a being of such power between them?

This profound shift in power dynamics promised to alter not only the course of the war between the kingdoms, but also the fate of all beings living under the rule of the elements.

Chapter XII: The Awakening Explosion

On the battlefield, a dense silence enveloped everyone present, interrupted only by the whispers of the wind that seemed to lament the recent events. The disappearance of "The Changeling" had left a palpable mark on the environment, a mixture of shock and emptiness that neither the fierce "The Firm One" nor the experienced Kaen could fill.

Kaen, regaining his composure despite his bewilderment, directed a meaningful glance toward "The Firm One". "Now, more than ever, we must stop it," he said, his voice firm but laden with uncertainty. Without waiting for a response, Kaen lunged once more at Fen, determined to end the conflict that had gone on for far too long.

However, as Kaen pounced, Fen, who was still in his berserk state, unleashed a massive explosion. The accumulated power, mixed with the essence of the Wind Dragon, erupted in a burst of pure energy that pushed Kaen and "The Firm One" back with devastating force.

The explosion left a smoking crater at its epicenter, and when the smoke began to clear, Fen stood, visibly confused but inexplicably composed. He seemed to have lost all sign of the powerful aura that had surrounded him moments before, but the most notable change was his appearance of calm and lucidity.

Fen looked around, trying to understand what had happened. He didn't clearly remember the events that led up to that moment, he only felt an immense power resonating within him, as if the forces of nature themselves had decided to lodge themselves in his soul.

Kaen and "The Firm One", still recovering from the impact, watched cautiously. The change in Fen was indisputable and disconcerting. Although he showed no signs of aggression, the mere fact that he had absorbed and then released so much energy so explosively kept them on guard.

The battlefield fell into a tense calm, each combatant sizing up the other, wondering what these new developments meant for the future of their kingdoms and the world at large. Fen, now standing in the center of the devastation he had caused, was beginning to understand the magnitude of what had happened, and the weight of responsibility that now fell on his shoulders was becoming more and more evident.

While the earth still resonated with the aftermath of the previous explosion, Fen, standing in the middle of the battlefield, was beginning to realize the depth of the change he had experienced. As Kaen bore down on him with indomitable ferocity, Fen, driven by a newfound instinct, reacted not with the familiar flow of water, but with a powerful, controlled gust of wind.

The air around Fen churned with an intensity reminiscent of "The Changeling" itself, forming a whirlpool that not only stopped Kaen in his tracks, but also pushed him back with astonishing force. Sand and dust rose in a whirlwind, creating a visual wall between Fen and Kaen.

Kaen, surprised and momentarily disoriented by the sudden manifestation of wind, attempted to readjust his focus. He looked at Fen, whose face revealed a mixture of surprise and gradual understanding. Fen looked at his own hands, almost as if he couldn't believe what he had just done.

"How is this possible?" Fen murmured, speaking more to himself than to his adversary. Confusion mingled with an emerging revelation. At that moment, a deeper understanding seemed to settle in his mind. ""The Changeling"... have you given me your strength?"

Up high, "The Firm One" watched the events unfold with an expression of concern and amazement. The power of the elements now clearly in play indicated a significant shift in the balance of the world that they, as dragons, had sworn to maintain.

Meanwhile, the battlefield stood in an expectant pause. Fen, now with the power of the wind at his disposal, felt energized and more powerful than ever. However, the gravity of the responsibility that this implied was beginning to weigh on him. Not only did he have to deal with the impending confrontation with Kaen, but he also needed to fully understand the legacy and sacrifice of "The Changeling".

His air still vibrant with power, Fen looked up at Kaen, who was regaining his position. "Kaen," Fen called, his voice carrying a new ring of authority and a hint of warning. "You must stop your attacks; we are no longer on the same level. I do not seek destruction, but I will defend with all necessary force."

Instead of answering directly, Kaen turned to "The Firm One", his eyes flashing with intense resolve. "Let's attack now, before we can no longer contain it!" he urged his ally. The determination in his voice reflected the urgency of the situation, knowing that if they let Fen get even stronger, he might become impossible to handle.

With renewed determination and power, Fen not only repelled every attempted attack from Kaen and "The Firm One" but also counterattacked with devastating force. Each attack of his was charged with the energy of the winds, each blow resonated with the authority of the Wind Dragon that was now part of his essence.

Kaen and "The Firm One" attempted to coordinate their attacks, looking for any opening, but Fen, with his new ability to manipulate the wind, created barriers and gusts that deflected each attempt. Fen's movements were fluid, almost ethereal, and his ability to anticipate and respond to his adversaries' attacks had been magnified exponentially.

As the battle dragged on, exhaustion began to take its toll on Kaen and "The Firm One" His movements, once precise and powerful, were now beginning to show signs of fatigue. Fen, on the other hand, seemed to be just getting started, his energy showing no signs of slowing down, fueled by the fusion with "The Changeling".

With "The Firm One" stunned by a particularly powerful gust of wind and Kaen recovering from a direct hit, Fen saw his opportunity. He raised his hands, the air around him humming with gathered power, and prepared to deliver what could be the final blow.

The air was charged with tension as Fen channeled all of his power into a single devastating attack. Kaen and "The Firm One", aware of the imminent threat, put themselves on guard, knowing that this could be the decisive moment of the battle.

Just as Fen was about to release his attack, the battlefield fell into an expectant silence. All eyes were on him, watching as the power of the wind condensed in his hands, ready to change the fate of everyone involved in this epic conflict.

The battlefield was charged with intense emotions; Fear, surprise, and amazement mingled in the air as Fen dominated the fight. However, at the climax of the battle, as Fen was about to deliver his final blow against Kaen and "The Firm One", the sky suddenly lit up with a blinding light.

From that dazzling light descended "The Glorious One", the Dragon of Light, a being of immense and mysterious power, whose existence was barely a whisper even among the most ancient dragons. His appearance was so unexpected that even "The Firm One" and Kaen stopped in their tracks, looking up with a mixture of reverence and fear.

"The Glorious One" did not utter a word. His presence alone emanated an absolute authority and power that resonated with the purity and strength of the primordial light. With a majestic movement, he raised a claw and a beam of pure light descended from the sky and struck directly at Fen.

The impact was so powerful that the ground beneath Fen fractured, creating a crater of enormous proportions where the warrior was trapped and immobilized. Dust and debris rose in a thick cloud, covering the scene with a veil of uncertainty.

As the dust settled, silence fell over the place. Kaen and "The Firm One", although relieved by the interruption, could not hide their bewilderment. The sudden turn of events left them wondering about "The Glorious one's" motivations for intervening in a conflict that seemed, until then, outside of their interest.

"The Glorious One" now floated over the battlefield, radiating a light that seemed to purify the air itself. There was no aggression in his actions, only a clear purpose and an overwhelming power that suggested that his participation in the battle was not an act of violence, but of necessity.

Now with everyone present watching in awe and awe of "The Glorious One", while Fen, slowly regaining his sense and strength, tried to understand the magnitude of what had just happened. The fate of the world and the balance of power had been irrevocably altered in an instant, under the gaze of a dragon whose mere presence defied all comprehension.

Fen, immobilized in the crater created by a new attack from "The Glorious One", felt a mixture of frustration and bewilderment as he watched the dragon of light prepare a new move. Although less devastating than the first, the impact was enough to keep him fixed in place, unable to get up or fight.

In those brief but eternal seconds, "The Glorious One" moved with supernatural speed. With a flash of light that illuminated the entire battlefield as if the sun itself were present, it took Kaen and "The Firm One" into its clutches. Without a word, the dragon of light quickly ascended into the sky, its radiance leaving a trail that cut the air like a knife.

Fen, despite his power and his new connection with "The Changeling", was helpless, his body unresponsive as the light that enveloped the trio disappeared over the horizon. His vision, through clouded by effort and pain, captured the last image of Kaen and "The Firm One" being carried away, perhaps to a fate or judgment he could not foresee.

As "The Glorious One" and his captives walked away, the battlefield began to darken. The intense light that had dominated the sky was fading, leaving behind only the twilight that was rapidly closing over the earth. It was as if, with the departure of "The Glorious One", the light of day itself withdrew, taking clarity with it and leaving behind unanswered questions and an uncertain future.

Fen, finally regaining some mobility, struggled to his feet. His mind was as agitated as his body; the sudden intervention of "The Glorious One", the disappearance of his adversaries, and the revelation of the power that now coursed through his veins were too much to process in the silence and darkness that now enveloped him.

Fen alone in the vast empty field, looking towards the place where "The Glorious One" had disappeared. Night had completely fallen, and with it, a heavy veil of uncertainty about what would come next. Fen knew that, despite the challenges overcome and the powers gained, his journey was far from over. The search for truth and justice continued, now in a world that seemed increasingly shrouded in shadows and mysteries.

In the twilight that followed the fight, Fen was alone, deep in thought. The sudden intervention of "The Glorious One" and the disappearance of Kaen and "The Firm One" had left a void both on the battlefield and in their understanding of recent events. As the silence of the night closed in on him, Fen meditated on the immense power he had experienced, a power he believed to have been a manifestation of his unconsciousness and the help of the Wind Dragon.

Sitting on the land still disturbed by the battle, Fen watched the sun fall, feeling how darkness enveloped the world around him. It was a moment of deep introspection, where doubts and uncertainty about his ability to handle the new power that resided in him were beginning to take shape.

"I must learn to control this force," he promised himself. "Not only for my own sake, but to ensure that the chaos I have experienced is not repeated. I need to use this power not for revenge, but to protect."

With renewed determination, Fen practiced wielding his elemental abilities under the cover of night. First, he tried to channel the wind, feeling it subtly respond to his desires. Then, he concentrated on the water, trying to shape and direct it with his will, seeking the calm necessary to dominate it.

Each small success gave him a greater understanding of how to balance the forces that were now a part of him. Although aware of the long road ahead, Fen felt increasingly prepared to face the challenges ahead.

As the night wore on, Fen looked up at the starry sky. The constellations offered him a sense of perspective and possibility. Although the path forward was filled with uncertainties, the view of the cosmos reminded him that his struggle was part of something much larger.

Now with Fen rising to his feet, his figure silhouetted against the night sky, a mute witness to his strengthened resolve. With the powers of water and wind at his disposal, he was ready to continue his search for truth and justice, not only for himself but for the balance of the entire world. Their journey, marked by learning and adaptation, continued under the sky, guided by the light of the stars and the promise of a new dawn.

Chapter XIII: In Search of the Dark One

Despite his mastery over the powers of water and wind, Fen was fully aware of the limitations he faced if several dragons or warriors like Kaen decided to join forces against him. The victory he had achieved earlier, although significant, was due in part to the fatigue and surprise of his adversaries, and was not indicative that he would always emerge victorious, especially now that "The Glorious One" seemed to have joined them.

"The Glorious One" was an entity whose magnificence and power eclipsed all the dragons Fen had met thus far. The power emanating from this being was overwhelming, and Fen knew that in a direct confrontation with it and other united dragons, his chances of success would be dramatically reduced.

With these thoughts occupying his mind, Fen decided that his best course of action was to seek an alliance or mentorship with "The Dark One", a being shrouded in mystery and ancient legends. Little was known about "The Dark One" in modern times, but ancient stories painted him as an entity of formidable power, possibly the only one capable of equaling or even surpassing "The Glorious One".

The search for "The Dark One" would not be easy or risk-free. Fen knew that this mysterious being had been avoided or even feared by many due to its enigmatic nature and the dark stories surrounding its existence. However, the desperate situation requires desperate measures, and Fen was willing to go down any path that would lead to a better understanding and mastery of his abilities, as well as a chance to protect the balance of the world.

Armed with determination and the knowledge that each step brought him closer to his destiny, Fen began to prepare for the search for "The Dark One". He knew this journey would take him through unknown and possibly dangerous terrain, but it was also a necessary part of his evolution as a warrior and as a guardian of world balance.

With dawn bearing witness to his resolve, Fen set out, leaving behind the relative safety of the known territory to venture into the unknown, where the answers to his deepest questions awaited him. It was the beginning of a new chapter in their journey, one that could define the future of the world.

Fen, guided by legends and rumors spread during his travels, set out on an exhaustive quest to find "The Dark One". He crossed desolate lands and stormy seas, exploring every corner that could harbor this enigmatic being. Eventually, his search took him to a remote island, a place distant from any known civilization, where the call became irresistible.

Convinced that the answer to his calling lay beneath the waves, Fen dove into the deep waters. The darkness of the ocean enveloped him as he descended into the unknown, increasingly convinced that he was close to his goal. The current guided him to a hidden and mysterious underwater cave, where the feeling of presence was overwhelming.

Inside the cave, the darkness was total, and the silence felt like a pressure on his body. Fen explored the interior, his hands sliding over the cold, damp surfaces of the rock, searching for any sign or hint of "The Dark One". However, to his surprise and frustration, the cave seemed to be completely empty.

The intensity of the call he had felt was fading, leaving Fen confused and disoriented in the darkness. Had he been deceived by his own desires or was there something else he wasn't seeing? In that moment of doubt, he began to question his journey, his purpose, and the true power he sought.

As Fen reflected in the stillness of the abyss, a cold current passed through him, like a whisper on water, hinting that the presence he sought might be something different from what he had imagined.

After moments of uncertainty in the underwater cave, the darkness began to move, coalescing into a figure that gradually took shape in front of Fen. "The Dark One" emerged, the Dragon of Darkness, whose presence felt both imposing and enigmatic. His eyes, an abyss within the abyss, fixed their gaze on Fen with an intensity that cut through the underwater silence.

"I know your quest, Fen," "The Dark One" began in a voice that resonated like a distant echo. "I have watched from the shadows, seeing beyond what mortal eyes can see. And I warn you, what you seek may tear the veil of your reality."

Fen, although shocked by the appearance, maintained his composure and expressed his resolve. "I need to know the truth, no matter how deep or disturbing. It's the only way left."

"The Dark One", moving with a fluidity that defied the logic of the water around them, moved closer to Fen. "The truth you seek will challenge you, question every battle you have fought, every alliance you have forged, and every enemy you have faced. Not only will it change your perception of the past, but it will also irrevocably alter your future course."

The seriousness of "The Dark One's" words weighed in the air, each syllable vibrating with the power of hidden truth. Fen felt his determination meet the uncertainty of the unknown. Was he really prepared to face a truth that could crumble everything he had believed in?

"I'm ready," Fen stated, his voice firm despite the doubts that plagued him. "Show me what I need to see, so I can understand and face what is coming."

With a slow approval, "The Dark One" extended one of his claws toward Fen. "So, prepare to face the shadows of the truth. You will not only see reality, you will experience it, and I assure you that the path forward will be both revealing and transformative."

So, in the forgotten depths of the world, Fen prepared to receive the answers he had so desperately sought, unaware that these revelations would be the catalyst for a transformation deeper than he had ever imagined.

As "The Dark One" prepared to reveal the truth, a soft blue glow emanated from Fen's body, visible only to the dragon who had before him the ability to see beyond the visible. The bluish aura, pulsing with an unknown rhythm, seemed to be indicative of incomplete preparation or internal resistance towards the truths that were about to be revealed.

"The Dark One" paused, carefully observing the light that enveloped Fen. "You are not fully prepared to face what is to come," he expressed in a deep voice that echoed in the depths of the underwater cave. Fen, surprised and confused, looked down at his own body, trying to see what the dragon saw, but to no avail.

"The Dark One's" decision was clear in his mind. He couldn't just reveal the truth to Fen like he had initially planned. Instead, he opted for a more radical and protective approach. "We must strengthen you further, not only in power, but in understanding and ability to accept the truth that could break many," the dragon explained.

Fen, although overwhelmed, nodded determinedly. "I will do whatever it takes. I trust your judgment."

With a solemn gesture, "The Dark One" outlined an enigmatic circle on the floor of the cave with a claw. Within the circle, ancient symbols began to appear, each glowing with a dark glow. "This is an ancient ritual, similar to the one "The Pacific" performed on you," the dragon said. "However, rather than simple preparation, this fusion will strengthen you and prepare you to face and endure what is coming without it consuming you."

Fen, following the instructions of "The Dark One", positioned himself in the center of the circle. The air was filled with electricity, and the water around them seemed to vibrate with the energy of the ritual. "This process will change you," "The Dark One" warned. "But it is necessary so that you can face what is coming and act accordingly."

With everything in place, "The Dark One" raised his claws towards the dark ceiling of the cave, and energy began to concentrate around both of them. Fen closed his eyes, preparing for what was to come, as the dragon began the ritual that would define the course of future events. The cave was filled with overwhelming power, just before the ritual began in earnest.

As dark energy swirled around them, "The Dark One" began to murmur ancient chants, the words echoing against the walls of the cave with an echo that seemed to come from another world. Fen, situated in the center of the mystical circle, felt how the dark power completely enveloped him, penetrating every cell of his being.

"Relax and let yourself be carried away by the flow of energy,"
"The Dark One" instructed in a voice that now sounded more like
an ethereal whisper than a physical voice. Fen obeyed, releasing
any tension in his body and mind, allowing the ritual to transform
him from the inside.

As the ritual progressed, the blue light emanating from Fen
became more intense and vibrant. In that moment, "The Dark
One" spoke directly to Fen's consciousness, not with words, but
through a deep connection that transcended human language.
He revealed to him that the blue light was a sign of his yet
unrealized potential and the challenges he would face in fully
controlling the power that was now fused with his soul.

The cave was illuminated with a surreal light, and Fen could see
reflections of his past and possible futures projected on the rock
walls. It was as if each symbol and each line of the circle told a
different story, a piece of the great puzzle of his destiny.

"The Dark One" continued the ritual, increasing the intensity of his magic. Fen began to feel an overwhelming pressure, as if he were being pulled toward a truth he had been afraid to face. The dark energy, although powerful and terrifying, also brought with it a sense of clarity and purpose.

"You are about to discover truths that many have sought and few have found," said "The Dark One" as the power reached its peak. "This knowledge may be a burden, but it is also the path to true liberation."

With a final surge of energy, the ritual reached its climax. A flash of dark light exploded around them, and Fen felt as if he were passing through an invisible barrier. When the light dissipated, he found himself standing, still in the circle, but transformed. His body and mind now housed the power and wisdom of the Dragon of Darkness, ready to face what was coming.

Silence settled in the cave once again, with "The Dark One" observing Fen with a look that mixed approval and seriousness. "Now you are ready to face your destiny," the dragon concluded, marking the end of the ritual and the beginning of a new stage in Fen's life.

The ritual completed and the fusion consummated left Fen with a sense of renewal and purpose. As "The Dark One" faded, his essence fully integrated into Fen, speaking to him in a mental whisper that only he could perceive. "Return to the place where you were once happy," the voice echoed in his mind, guiding him towards his old home.

With his resolve fixed and new powers pulsing through his veins, Fen emerged from the underwater cave and rose toward the surface. The water swirled around him, obeying his newfound wills and allowing him to cut through the ocean with supernatural speed. The sea currents assisted him, and the creatures of the sea moved away from him, recognizing the strength he now carried.

The island where he had lived with his family was now desolate and abandoned, a grim reminder of happier times. Upon arriving, Fen felt a wave of longing and pain mixed with determination.

Every step he took through the land of his childhood resonated with echoes of the past and the potential future that "The Dark One" had hinted at.

Exploring the ruins of what was once his home, Fen began to feel a deeper connection to the place. Memories of laughter and love filled the air, but so did whispers of buried secrets and hidden truths. Fen walked slowly through the remains of his old life, touching the time-worn objects that had once been part of his daily life.

As he entered what was left of his house, a particular glow caught his attention. Under a damaged wooden floor, he found an ancient chest, covered in dust and algae, that seemed to have been sheltered from the rest of the world for years. With a wave of his hand, Fen cleaned the chest and opened it, discovering within several artifacts and an ancient manuscript written in a language that only "The Dark One" could have prepared him to understand.

The symbols on the manuscript began to glow as Fen touched them, each touch revealing more of the hidden history of his family and the kingdoms. The voice of "The Dark One", now a part of his consciousness, explained to him the meanings and secrets that those symbols contained.

Thus, with each page of the manuscript, Fen discovered more about his family's true purpose, his connection to the dragons, and the true reasons behind the war between the kingdoms. What began as a journey in search of revenge was turning into a mission to discover the truth and, perhaps, to find a way to restore peace and balance to a world torn by conflict and misunderstanding.

With the manuscript in hand and the revelations still reverberating in his mind, Fen prepared to decode the last part of the ancient document. As his eyes traveled over the last few lines, an unexpected detail caught his attention, something so surprising that it made him question everything he had learned up to that point. Fen remained motionless, staring at the manuscript, a mixture of disbelief and anticipation appearing on his face.

Chapter XIV: The Council in the Celestial Kingdom

While Fen dived into the depths in search of "The Dark One", in another part of the world, "The Glorious One" transported Kaen and "The Firm One" to his kingdom in the sky. This celestial realm, a place of unparalleled beauty and resplendent light, extended beyond the clouds, where the atmosphere was filled with an ethereal peace. Here, Kaen and "The Firm One's" physical and emotional wounds began to heal, although the memory of the fierce battle against Fen and the tragic loss of "The Changeling" remained fresh in their minds.

Kaen and "The Firm One" were received with the majestic hospitality of the celestial kingdom, where the radiance of pure light bathed everything around them. Their bodies, exhausted and battered by the recent conflict, found rest in a sanctuary of peace and recovery. However, they knew that downtime was limited; the balance of the world was at stake, and crucial decisions had to be made.

Once recovered, "The Glorious One" summoned them to a radiant chamber, whose walls shone with the light of a thousand suns. Kaen and "The Firm One" walked together down a long white marble hallway, whose surfaces reflected their passage. The solemnity of the place and the importance of the meeting weighed on them.

Upon arrival, they were greeted by the imposing figure of "The Glorious One", whose presence illuminated the vast chamber. The Dragon of Light, with its aura of purity and power, exuded an authoritative calm. His eyes, which seemed to contain all the knowledge and wisdom of the cosmos, were fixed on Kaen and "The Firm One".

"Thank you for coming," "The Glorious One" began, his voice echoing like soft thunder in the vast chamber. "We face an unprecedented threat. Fen's fusion with "The Changeling" and "The Pacific" has given rise to a power we cannot underestimate. We must decide the course of our actions before it is too late."

Kaen and "The Firm One" listened attentively, understanding the seriousness of the situation. The atmosphere was charged with tension as they processed the words of "The Glorious One". They both knew that the fate of the world depended on the decisions they made in that heavenly chamber.

"The Glorious One" continued, his voice firm and full of authority. "Our unity is crucial. Together, we must find a way to restore balance and prevent Fen from causing further destruction. His power is immense, but if we act with wisdom and strategy, we can prevail."

The conversation continued, full of strategies, discussions and plans. The fate of the world depended on the decisions they made in that heavenly chamber. "The Glorious One" knew that time was of the essence, and that the upcoming confrontation with Fen would be decisive for the future of all kingdoms.

Determination grew stronger in each of them as they prepared to face the challenge that awaited them. High in the sky, in the resplendent celestial realm, Kaen, "The Firm One" and "The

Glorious One" were ready to make a momentous decision, one that could change the fate of the world forever.

In the brilliant celestial chamber, where the light of "The Glorious One" illuminated every corner, "The Firm One" took the floor to present his vision on how they should proceed in the face of the threat that Fen represented. His voice, deep and resonant like the echo in the caverns, filled the space with a mixture of conviction and strategy.

"I think our best option is to face Fen together, as a united force," "The Firm One" began, looking at "The Glorious one" and Kaen. "We must combine our powers and abilities to overwhelm him. Fen has proven to be incredibly strong, but he is not invincible. If we work together, we can defeat him."

Kaen nodded slightly, recognizing the logic in "The Firm One's" words. "Continue," he said, inviting the dragon to detail his plan.

"First, we must lure Fen to a terrain where we have the advantage," "The Firm One" explained. "A place where we can maximize our forces and minimize theirs. A terrain with characteristics that favor our elements. We can use my control over the land to create barriers and traps, limiting their movements and channeling their attacks into specific areas."

"The Glorious One" nodded, his eyes shining with interest. "And what do you propose we do once we have him on that land?"

"We can wear him down slowly, using combined attacks to deplete his energy," "The Firm One" continued. "Kaen, your fire skills can keep him at bay and force him to expend his energy on defenses. "The Glorious One", your light can blind and disorient him, creating opportunities for more precise and powerful attacks."

Kaen considered the strategy. "And how do you think we should handle the essence of "The Pacific" and "The Changeling"?"

"Once we have weakened him enough, we can try to separate "The Pacific" from his body," "The Firm One" explained. "With the help of our combined powers, we can rip the essence of "The

Pacific" from within and return it to the realm of water, where it should be."

"And "The Changeling"?" "The Glorious One" asked, his tone filled with curiosity and caution.

"We can try to extract the essence of "The Changeling" and return it to the realm of air," "The Firm One" replied. "There, the nobles and sages of the air can decide who would be the best candidate to absorb that power and continue their legacy. It is crucial that each essence return to its place of origin, maintaining balance between the kingdoms."

The chamber fell silent as Kaen and "The Glorious One" processed "The Firm One's" words. His plan was bold and complex, but it made sense. Fen represented a threat they could not ignore, and the only way to deal with it was with a well-thought-out strategy and unprecedented collaboration.

"It's an ambitious plan," Kaen admitted. "But it has merit. We must consider all options and prepare for any eventuality. The key will be coordination and precision in our attacks."

"The Glorious One" nodded, his eyes shining with a renewed light. "If we all agree, we can proceed with this strategy. But first, we must listen to all opinions and consider any other perspectives before making a final decision."

"The Firm One's" plan was now on the table, waiting to be discussed and refined by the other members of the heavenly council. The battle against Fen promised to be one of the most difficult they had ever faced, but with unity and determination, they believed they could restore balance and prevent the world from falling into chaos.

The atmosphere in the heavenly chamber became even more tense when "The Glorious One" spoke. His voice resonated with an authoritative calm, befitting someone who had observed the world from above, watching the threads of fate intertwine and unravel.

"I have a proposal that may seem radical," "The Glorious One" began, his luminous eyes settling on "The Firm One" and Kaen. "But it is one that, in my heart, I believe is the only way to achieve the lasting peace that we have longed for since time immemorial. My proposal is that all dragons, we, sacrifice ourselves and give our power to a single human being. "

The silence that followed his words was absolute. "The Firm One" and Kaen looked at "The Glorious One" in amazement and confusion.

"What are you saying?" Kaen asked, trying to understand the magnitude of what "The Glorious One" was suggesting.

"The Glorious One" continued, his gaze firm and determined. "A long time ago, I had a meeting with "The Wild One". We talked about the conflicts that plague our world and the possible solutions. It was then that "The Wild One" revealed an idea to me: the only way to achieve true and lasting peace. It would be for the dragons to disappear, sacrificing our existence to give our power to a single human being who could maintain balance and protect the world in our place."

Kaen stayed silent, processing what he had just heard. The idea of all the dragons sacrificing themselves was inconceivable, but at the same time, there was a logic to it that he couldn't deny. "The Glorious One" continued, looking at Kaen with an intensity that seemed to penetrate his soul.

"The Wild One" told me that he had waited because he knew that in the kingdom of fire a suitable person would be born to fulfill that purpose," explained "The Glorious One". "A person with the heart and strength to bear the weight of such responsibility. That person, Kaen, is you."

Kaen felt the weight of those words fall on him like a stone. "The Firm One" observed in silence, assimilating the radical proposal of "The Glorious one"".

"If we accept this proposal," "The Glorious One" continued, "our powers combined into a single being could bring the peace we have longed for. We could avoid further conflict and ensure that balance is maintained for future generations."

The chamber remained in deep silence, each one of them contemplating the magnitude of "The Glorious One's" proposal. The thought of sacrificing himself to grant his power to a single human was daunting, but the promise of lasting peace was tempting.

Kaen, with a heavy heart, wondered if he could really be the person destined to carry such a burden. Meanwhile, "The Firm One" was torn between his loyalty to the principles of the dragons and the possibility of a new future under a single human protector.

The fate of the world was at stake, and the decisions they made at that moment would define the course of history forever.

Kaen remained silent, weighing the proposals presented before him. His mind ran over every word of "The Glorious one" and "The Firm One" aware of the magnitude of what was at stake.

The weight of the world's fate seemed to rest on his shoulders. Finally, he looked up and spoke with a serenity that reflected his inner determination.

"I only wish to honor "The Wild One's" wish: to achieve true peace," Kaen stated, his voice firm and determined. "I don't know if I'm the one chosen to carry this burden, but if you dragons trust me, I won't let you down."

"The Firm One", who had observed Kaen with a mix of skepticism and curiosity, felt a growing empathy for the human. Kaen's determination and humility could not be ignored. However, his experience and prudence dictated that he could not so easily accept such a drastic proposal without ensuring that Kaen was truly prepared for such a responsibility.

"If you truly wish to be the bearer of our essence and power," said "The Firm One", his voice resonating with the gravity of the decision they were about to make, "you must pass a series of tests. These tests will not only measure your strength and abilities, but also your heart and spirit."

Kaen nodded, ready to face any challenge that came his way. "I am prepared. Tell me what these tests are and I will face them."

The Earth Dragon, seeing the determination in the eyes of the one who was previously a simple man, could not help but feel a growing empathy and respect. The proposal of "The Glorious One" still weighed on his mind, but the possibility that Kaen could overcome these tests and prove himself gave him a ray of hope.

"If you pass these tests," "The Firm One" continued, "I will be willing to sacrifice my existence and carry out what "The Glorious One" has proposed. The fate of peace is at stake, and these tests will determine whether you are truly worthy. to carry the power of the dragons and carry out our mission."

Kaen nodded, understanding the seriousness of what was being asked of him. He knew these trials would not be easy, but he was determined to face any obstacle to achieve true peace and honor the legacy of "The Wild One". With a look of determination and confidence, he prepared to face the trials that would define not only his destiny, but the destiny of the entire world.

Kaen stood on the threshold of a monumental challenge. The words of "The Firm One" echoed in his mind as he prepared for the first test. He felt the weight of responsibility, but also the strength he had gained throughout his journey. His determination was unwavering, and he knew that he must succeed not only for himself, but for all those who trusted him.

Chapter XV: The Trials of Kaen

The atmosphere in the heavenly realm was charged with tension. "The Glorious One", the Dragon of Light, visibly disagreed with "The Firm One's" proposal. With a stern look, he tried to dissuade Kaen from accepting the evidence.

"You should not accept these conditions," said "The Glorious One" firmly. "If you sacrifice yourself using the power of fire and light, you could subdue "The Firm One" and force him to give up his essence. There is no need for these tests."

Kaen stared into the eyes of "The Glorious One". There was a mixture of determination and serenity in his eyes. "There is no need to resort to violence," Kaen replied calmly. "I want to earn the trust and respect of "The Firm One". If I have to go through these tests to prove myself, I will."

"The Glorious One" hesitated, but the firmness in Kaen's voice left no room for doubt. Finally, he relented, although his expression clearly showed his concern. "Very well," he said with resignation, "but don't forget what's at stake."

"The Firm One" nodded, grateful for Kaen's decision. "Very well, Kaen. The tests you must pass will be three, and each one will test a different aspect of you."

"First," continued "The Firm One" "the test of strength and endurance. You must face a formidable enemy in direct combat. Without using the power of the fire that resides in you, only your human strength."

Kaen nodded, feeling the weight of the first test. He knew that his physical strength would be tested like never before.

"Second," the Earth Dragon continued, "the test of wisdom. You must solve an ancient riddle that has baffled wise men for centuries. This test will test your mind and your ability to think beyond the obvious."

Kaen knew he would need to focus and use all his wits to overcome this challenge. Wisdom hadn't always been his strong point, but he was willing to prove himself.

"And finally," said "The Firm One" gravely, "the test of the heart. You must demonstrate your ability to sacrifice yourself for the greater good, facing a situation that will test your values and your ability to make difficult decisions. This test will not be revealed until you overcome the first two."

Kaen nodded again, knowing that this last challenge would be the most difficult of all. The true test of a leader was not in his strength or his intelligence, but in his ability to make sacrifices for the good of others.

With the evidence established, "The Firm One" and "The Glorious One" watched Kaen, awaiting his final response. "I accept this evidence," Kaen stated firmly. "I will overcome them not only for myself, but for all those who trust in me and for the future of our kingdoms."

The Dragon of Light watched with concern as "The Firm One" nodded, satisfied with Kaen's response. The fate of the world hung in the balance, and the trials Kaen was about to face would determine the path to true peace or inevitable conflict.

Kaen stood at the foot of a towering mountain that rose majestically into the sky. The first test that "The Firm One" had assigned him consisted of traveling a distance of more than 300 kilometers to reach the summit in less than a day. At first, Kaen was surprised, believing that the challenge was a direct confrontation. However, there was no time for doubts, and he prepared to begin the ascent with iron determination.

Kaen ran with impressive speed, relying on his human strength and endurance. The mountainous landscape was rugged, but it did not seem to be an insurmountable challenge. However, as he moved forward, Kaen began to notice something strange. The terrain around him seemed to shift and shift unnaturally. Rocks were sliding, paths were suddenly blocked, and new routes opened in unexpected directions.

Pausing for a moment to take a closer look, Kaen realized that these changes were no coincidence. They were being controlled. He quickly deduced that it was "The Firm One" who manipulated the terrain to test his tenacity and skills. The Earth Dragon would not simply allow him to advance, and the real confrontation was overcoming these natural and artificial obstacles.

Kaen then understood that he had to beat "The Firm One" at his own game. Far from giving up, he redoubled his efforts. Using all his skill and adaptability, Kaen navigated obstacles with ingenuity and brute strength when necessary. Every step was a battle against the shifting terrain, but his determination did not waver.

As time passed, the challenge became more exhausting. The hours passed quickly, and the top of the mountain still seemed far away. However, Kaen refused to give up. With each obstacle overcome, his conviction grew stronger. He knew that this test was not only a test of his physical endurance, but also his mental and spiritual strength.

Finally, after a titanic effort, Kaen reached the top of the mountain just before time ran out. Exhausted but victorious, he allowed himself a brief moment to catch his breath. He knew he had passed the first test, but there was no time to relax. The second challenge awaited him, and he had to be prepared.

"You have shown great strength and endurance," "The Firm One" said, his voice echoing through the cold mountain air. "But the next test will be different. You must enter the center of this mountain and solve the enigma it holds. To do so, you must merge with the mountain through meditation."

Kaen nodded, accepting the new challenge. However, he knew that the wisdom test would be even more complicated. Determined to continue forward, he began to descend a hidden path that would take him to the heart of the mountain. In his mind, he reviewed everything he had learned and experienced, preparing to face the enigma that awaited him in the depths.

The second test of Kaen was in the heart of a mountain that held an ancient enigma. This mountain was famous for challenging sages and scholars over the centuries, none of whom had managed to solve its mystery. All those who tried to decipher the enigma died in the attempt, trapped by the internal collapse of the mountain that did not let anything or anyone out.

Kaen entered the mountain, remembering the words of "The Firm One". He knew that the key to solving the riddle was not brute force or simple intelligence, but something deeper. As he moved toward the center, the mountain began to close around him, its walls narrowing and the ground shaking, threatening to collapse.

Upon reaching the center, Kaen sat down and closed his eyes. He began to meditate, just as "The Firm One" had instructed him. Breathing deeply, he let his mind empty and focused on the sensations around him. I felt the earth, the rocks, the very energy of the mountain. He allowed himself to blend into his surroundings, feeling every little vibration, every movement of the rocks.

As the mountain walls continued to close in and rocks fell, Kaen remained motionless. His mind went deeper and deeper into the core of the mountain. That's when he started to understand. The riddle of the mountain was nothing more than an illusion, a mental trap designed to disorient and confuse those who sought to solve it.

Concentrating fully, Kaen visualized the mountain as an extension of his own being. He stood up with his eyes still closed and began to walk in a straight line, guided by his instinct and the deep connection he had established with the mountain. Even though there seemed to be no visible exit, he continued to move forward with determination.

Every step he took made the mountain shake, but Kaen did not stop. With unwavering faith, he created a large entrance in the rock. The walls opened before him, as if responding to his will. The light from outside began to filter through the new opening he had created, and Kaen emerged from the mountain, his eyes still closed.

When he opened them, he saw "The Firm One" and "The Glorious One" waiting for him. The two dragons watched him with a mixture of amazement and respect. Kaen had passed the second test not only with intelligence, but also with a deep and sincere connection to the land.

"You have shown a wisdom and strength that few possess," said "The Firm One" with admiration. "You are ready to face the third and final test. This will be the most difficult of all and will test your heart and your determination."

Kaen nodded, mentally preparing himself for the final challenge. He knew that his destiny was about to be defined and that the future of the world depended on his success in this final test.

Kaen stood before "The Firm One" and "The Glorious One", ready to face the final challenge. "The Firm One", with a stern look, explained to him what the last test consisted of: he had to face the Earth Dragon using only his human strength and abilities, without resorting to any extra power.

"This will be the most difficult test," warned "The Firm One". "You must defeat me without using the powers within you. Only your human strength and will."

"The Glorious One" again expressed his discontent. "This is crazy," he said, his voice booming like thunder. "No human can face a dragon without extra powers. Kaen, refuse this test. You cannot win."

Kaen, with a determined look, looked "The Glorious One" in the eyes and responded firmly. "Do not stand in the way. I am determined to pass this test, not only to prove myself, but to show that the human will can be as powerful as any magic or supernatural force. I will face "The Firm One" and defeat him with nothing more than my strength and my determination."

"The Glorious One" was stunned by Kaen's determination, but eventually stepped aside, allowing the fight to begin.

Kaen felt a surge of emotions as he prepared for the confrontation. He knew that facing a dragon without using his powers was a monumental challenge, but it was also an opportunity to demonstrate his inner strength. He closed his eyes for a moment, breathing deeply and remembering all the lessons he had learned throughout his life. The image of his family, the sacrifice of "The Wild One", and the countless confrontations he had overcome, gave him the determination he needed.

"The Firm One", for his part, observed Kaen with a mixture of respect and curiosity. He had underestimated humans before, but he knew that Kaen was different. The decision to undergo this test, without resorting to the strength of the fire within him, showed a bravery and determination that was worthy of admiration. However, he had no intention of going easy on him.

This test was to prove that Kaen had what it took to carry the weight of the world on his shoulders.

The Earth Dragon mentally prepared for combat. He knew better than to underestimate Kaen, even though he was at a disadvantage. The real test was not only physical strength, but also mental and emotional endurance.

The air around was charged with tension. "The Glorious One", although reluctant, stepped aside to allow the test to take place. His golden gaze followed Kaen's every movement, every breath. There was palpable concern in his eyes, but also a spark of curiosity to see how this confrontation would play out.

Kaen adopted a fighting stance, his muscles tense and ready to react. He felt the weight of expectation on his shoulders, but he didn't let it daunt him. Instead, he used that pressure to strengthen his resolve. He knew the enormous strength of "The Firm One" and knew that he would have to be cunning and precise in his movements.

"The Firm One" also positioned himself, his immense body radiating power and stability. Every fiber of his being was tuned for combat. He looked at Kaen, assessing his stance and preparing for the first exchange.

The silence between them was dense, broken only by the whisper of the wind and the slight tremor of the earth beneath their feet. Both contenders were ready, and the final battle that would decide everyone's fate was about to begin.

The battlefield was set, and the tension was palpable. Kaen and "The Firm One" stared at each other, each aware of the magnitude of the confrontation that was about to begin. The winds swirled around them, and the ground beneath their feet seemed to vibrate with anticipation. Without further ado, "The Firm One" launched the first attack.

The Earth Dragon lunged forward with devastating force, its claws and fangs gleaming with deadly menace. Each blow was like the impact of a mountain, and Kaen had to use all his agility and dexterity to dodge the attacks. He knew that a single well-aimed blow could end the battle in an instant.

Kaen backed away, jumping and rolling to avoid "The Firm One's" attacks. The dragon's strength seemed unstoppable, and every movement of its body made the earth shake. However, Kaen was not intimidated. He maintained his concentration, searching for an opening, a moment of weakness in the dragon's powerful defense.

Time passed, and the intensity of the battle did not decrease. Kaen, although exhausted, continued forward. Every time it looked like "The Firm One" was going to defeat him, Kaen found a way to dodge or block the blow. His movements were quick and precise, demonstrating unwavering determination.

Finally, Kaen saw his chance. In a moment of "The Firm One's" distraction, Kaen lunged forward with astonishing speed. His hand, holding a makeshift spear, moved with surgical precision. He managed to find a small space between the dragon's powerful scales and stabbed the spear with all his strength.

"The Firm One" roared in pain and retreated, surprised by the unexpected attack. But Kaen did not stop. He continued to launch a series of attacks, using his wits and skill to hurt the earth dragon. Each blow was calculated to weaken the powerful opponent, and soon "The Firm One" began to show signs of fatigue and serious injuries.

Despite the pain and fatigue, Kaen showed no signs of stopping. He knew he had to keep going, prove his worth and his ability to face any challenge. But just as he was about to deliver the final blow, he stopped. He raised his hand, indicating that enough was enough.

"I have already proven myself," Kaen said, his voice firm and clear. "There is no need to continue fighting. If you are not satisfied with what you have seen, join me as an ally in the battle to come. Together, we can face any threat and protect this world."

"The Firm One" stood still, his breathing heavy and his eyes fixed on Kaen. For a moment, the battlefield was silent, and everyone present waited for the dragon's response.

Kaen, still breathing heavily from the intense combat, turned on his heel and began walking towards "The Glorious One". His upright posture and the determined gleam in his eyes were testament to his victory and his unwavering resolve. He knew that fighting Fen would require more than just courage and determination; he needed the combined power of the dragons to triumph.

"I'm ready," he told "The Glorious One" with a firm voice. "It's time for me to receive your essence to defeat Fen once and for all."

As Kaen approached, "The Firm One" stayed behind, his imposing figure showing signs of exhaustion and reflection. Defeated by a mere human, he finally understood that his time in this world had come to an end. Humanity, with its ability to overcome seemingly insurmountable obstacles, was ready to lead the future.

With a shout that echoed throughout the battlefield, "The Firm One" called to Kaen. "Wait! If you are going to lead this world, you must be complete. I will be the first to sacrifice myself and give you my entire being and essence."

Kaen stopped and turned to face the Earth Dragon. "The Firm One" advanced with solemn dignity, each step an acknowledgment of the new era that was about to begin. Arriving in front of Kaen, the dragon bowed its enormous head in respect.

"You have shown a strength and determination that only a few possess," said "The Firm One" "It is time for my power to strengthen you for the final challenge."

A green and golden glow enveloped the Earth Dragon as the transfer ritual began. Kaen felt a surge of energy coursing through his body, a deep connection to the earth and its elements. The ground beneath his feet trembled and then stabilized, as if the earth itself welcomed its new guardian.

"The Firm One" let out a final breath as his essence merged with Kaen's, becoming an intrinsic part of his being. Kaen now held the power of Earth and Fire, his body strengthened and his spirit more determined than ever.

With a new and powerful determination, Kaen turned his gaze towards "The Glorious One". "I am ready to receive your essence. Together, we will defeat Fen and restore balance."

"The Glorious One" nodded slowly, acknowledging the sacrifice of "The Firm One" and the immense burden Kaen was willing to carry. The final battle was approaching, and with each new strength Kaen gained, he came closer to fulfilling his destiny.

Chapter XVI: Preparation for the Final Battle

With the power of "The Firm One" and "The Wild One" fused within him, Kaen was on the verge of completing his ultimate transformation. At his side, "The Glorious One" prepared for his final sacrifice, knowing that his essence would be the key to balancing the power Kaen needed to confront Fen.

Just as "The Glorious One" began the ritual, they both felt a disturbance in the air. Fen's fusion with "The Dark One" was complete, unleashing a torrent of energy that resonated through all the realms. Fen now possessed the powers of water, wind, and darkness, making his presence felt in every corner of the world.

"We must hurry," said "The Glorious One", his voice heavy with urgency. "The balance of the world is at stake, and we cannot allow darkness to prevail."

Before sacrificing himself, "The Glorious One" used his immense power to send a message to all corners of his kingdom and the kingdom of Earth. He summoned his subjects, urging them to seek shelter and prepare for the impending battle. His words resonated like an echo of hope and warning at the same time.

"Inhabitants of the realms of Light and Earth," "The Glorious One" proclaimed, his voice echoing in the hearts of all. "A great battle is coming, one that will endanger the very existence of our world. Take shelter and trust in Kaen, who will carry our legacy and guide us to a future of prosperity and unity. No more separate kingdoms, but one united world under one leader."

The inhabitants of both kingdoms, although fearful, accepted the truth of his words and prepared for the days to come. Kaen, now aware of the magnitude of his mission, was filled with new determination. He must not only defeat Fen, but also unite all the peoples under his leadership.

The ritual of "The Glorious one" reached its climax. A blinding glow enveloped the Dragon of Light, and its essence began to flow towards Kaen. The energy of light, pure and powerful, merged with the forces of fire and earth that already lived within it. Kaen felt as if the weight of worlds rested on his shoulders, but also a clarity and purpose he had never experienced.

Meanwhile, in the shadows, Fen felt the cold, overwhelming energy of darkness, combined with the fluidity of water and the freedom of wind. The two were destined to clash, and the world watched in fear and hope.

With the essence of "The Glorious One" finally absorbed, Kaen stood up, feeling complete. He was now the bearer of the powers of the three dragons, a symbol of unity and strength. The Dragon of Light, in his final act, had convinced the kingdoms to follow Kaen into a united future.

The final battle was about to begin, and with it, the fate of the world would be decided. Kaen and Fen, each wielding the power of three dragons, prepared to face each other in a duel that would echo through the centuries.

Kaen, determined to put an end to Fen's threat, decided not to waste any more time. With the powers of light, earth and fire fused into his being, he headed to the realm of water, where he knew Fen was. Upon arrival, what he witnessed was something he would never have imagined.

From a distance, Kaen watched as Fen was in a state of uncontrolled rage. His movements were erratic and violent, as if he were fighting an internal battle against invisible forces. As Kaen got closer, the scene became clearer and more terrifying. Fen seemed to be attacking himself, his face contorted into a grimace of pain and madness.

Kaen stopped, perplexed by what he saw. What had caused this state in Fen? Was it the power of darkness he had absorbed or something deeper? Questions swirled in his mind, but he had no answers. He could only watch, waiting for the right moment to intervene.

Suddenly, a dark aura surrounded Fen, and with a guttural scream, he expelled the Water Dragon, "The Pacific", from his body. The dragon, instead of looking dejected, was laughing sinisterly. Fen, with a sword of total darkness in his hands, launched himself at "The Pacific" and pierced it without mercy. The dragon essence was absorbed by the sword, and "The Pacific" disappeared in a whirlwind of shadows.

Kaen, stunned, could not fully understand what he was seeing. The darkness emanating from Fen was palpable, an evil presence that seemed to consume everything around him. The power of "The Pacific" had been devoured, and now Fen was more dangerous than ever.

Kaen's heart was filled with a mixture of fear and determination. He knew he had to stop Fen, but the dark power surrounding him was formidable. However, he remembered the words and sacrifices of the dragons who had entrusted him with their powers. He knew he had to face Fen, not only with strength, but also with wisdom and hope for a better future.

"Fen," Kaen called, his voice echoing through the chaos. "This doesn't have to end like this. You don't have to let the darkness consume you."

But Fen, his gaze lost in madness, showed no signs of listening. The sword of darkness in his hand vibrated with evil energy, and Kaen knew that the final showdown was about to begin.

With one last look of determination, Kaen prepared himself for what was to come. The battle between the bringer of light, earth and fire against the warrior of darkness, water and wind was about to decide the fate of their world.

In a matter of seconds, Fen charged towards Kaen with a ferocity and determination that only a warrior consumed by darkness could possess. His eyes burned with a deranged intensity, and each of his movements was imbued with overwhelming aggression. Kaen, on the other hand, stood his ground, with an unflappable calm that reflected his deep sense of responsibility and determination.

Fen, wielding his sword of utter darkness, unleashed a flurry of attacks with deadly precision. The blade moved like an extension of its own fury, leaving behind a trail of shadows that seemed to consume the light itself. Kaen, using the combined power of fire, earth and light, skillfully blocked and dodged each blow. A shield of sparkling light formed around him, deflecting the most dangerous attacks and dispelling the darkness that tried to envelop him.

To each attack from Fen, Kaen responded with impenetrable defenses. He used fire to counteract water, earth to absorb and neutralize gusts of wind, and light to dispel shadows. Each confrontation was a spectacle of pure elemental energy, with the battlefield transforming into an arena of controlled chaos.

Fen's madness and aggressiveness were becoming more and more evident. His thirst for revenge and the influence of the Dragon of Darkness led him to attack without respite, with almost animalistic brutality. Kaen, on the other hand, remained focused, using his power strategically and precisely. He knew he couldn't let himself get carried away by anger; Their mission was to protect and restore balance, not destroy.

The ground shook with each clash of their forces. Fen summoned whirlwinds of wind that raised enormous waves from the nearby sea, launching them towards Kaen with devastating force. Kaen responded with pillars of earth rising to block the impact, followed by bursts of fire that evaporated the water into a cloud of steam.

Despite his aggressiveness, Fen was unable to penetrate Kaen's defenses. Every attempted attack was repelled, and every blow delivered was absorbed by the power of the earth or dissipated by light. The battle continued in a tense balance, with Kaen playing defensively, patiently waiting for a mistake from Fen.

As the fighting intensified, Fen's fury turned to desperation. His attacks became more erratic, fueled by a mix of rage and frustration. Kaen, observing his opponent's movements, understood that the key to winning was not to match his fury, but to overcome it with serenity and precision.

The two warriors continued their dance of destruction and defense, with the fate of the world hanging in a delicate balance. In each clash of their powers, the battlefield transformed, reflecting the titanic confrontation between light and darkness, serenity and fury, hope and revenge.

And so, in the midst of a storm of unleashed elements, the final battle began to define not only the fate of Fen and Kaen, but the future of all the kingdoms they had known.

The battle continued, increasingly intense and devastating. Fen, his fury overflowing, attacked relentlessly, unleashing blasts of water, wind, and darkness with lethal precision. Kaen, maintaining his calm and control, countered with the power of fire, earth, and light. Each attack and defense caused explosions of energy that resonated throughout the island, destroying everything in its path.

The island, once a place of peace and happiness for Fen, was crumbling under the destructive power of battle. Trees fell, rocks disintegrated, and the ground fragmented into deep craters. However, Fen seemed indifferent to the destruction of his former home. His mind was clouded with fury and revenge, his only goal was to defeat Kaen.

Kaen, for his part, felt a responsibility to protect not only himself, but also Fen and the entire world. He knew he must stand his ground, that he could not allow himself to be swept away by the same darkness that consumed his opponent. Each time Fen launched an attack, Kaen responded with a calculated defense, absorbing and dissipating the destructive energy.

The intensity of the fighting reached unimaginable levels. Fen summoned a hurricane of wind and water, spinning with such force that it tore chunks of the island and threw them into the air. Kaen responded with a barrier of light that split the hurricane in two, creating a safe passage for him. Seizing the opportunity, he lunged toward Fen, trying to get close enough to speak to him, to try to break the darkness that enveloped him.

But Fen wasn't listening. His sword of darkness moved with inhuman speed and strength, constantly searching for Kaen. Each blow that Kaen managed to deflect created a burst of energy that destroyed more of the surroundings. The place that was once their home was transformed into a desolate battlefield.

In a moment of desperation, Fen unleashed all of his power, creating a sphere of pure darkness that began to expand, absorbing everything in its path. Kaen, realizing the magnitude of the attack, responded with an explosion of light that stopped the spread of darkness, creating a struggle of opposing energies in the center of the island.

The power unleashed by both warriors was such that the ground began to crack and the entire island began to sink into the ocean. The destruction was total, but Fen did not stop. He continued to attack, blinded by fury, while Kaen defended himself, seeking an opportunity to free Fen from his madness.

The battle seemed to have no end, and the destruction advanced without respite. Memories of the family and happiness that once inhabited that island were fading among the rubble, as Fen and Kaen continued their titanic confrontation. The fate of the world hung in the balance, and the final battle between these two warriors continued without a clear winner in sight.

The fight between the two warriors continued, with an intensity that seemed to have no end. Fen, consumed by his fury, launched attacks with unmatched ferocity. Kaen, despite the chaos around him, maintained his defense, trying to find a way to free Fen from the darkness that enveloped him.

As he blocked a powerful gust of wind and darkness, Kaen began to remember the first time he faced Fen. Back then, Fen was nothing more than a desperate man, searching for answers about the tragedy that had struck his family. Kaen remembered the look of pain and determination in Fen's eyes, an image that contrasted sharply with the rage-filled being before him.

Flashback:

Fen, with a face marked by sadness, appeared before Kaen in the kingdom of fire. "I just want to know what happened to my family," he had said, his voice shaky but firm. Kaen, though reluctant at first, had seen the sincerity in Fen's eyes and felt a connection, a mutual understanding of the pain within.

Returning to the present, Kaen saw glimpses of that same person in Fen's movements, in his desperate struggle. Every attack he launched, every defense he executed, seemed charged with an anguish that only someone who has lost everything could understand.

The battle raged on, the island crumbling beneath their feet, but Kaen couldn't help but see through Fen's fury and remember the man who once sought the truth. "Fen," Kaen shouted over the din of battle, "this is not what you wanted. Remember who you were. Remember why you started all of this."

But Fen didn't seem to listen. His attacks became even more frantic, as if Kaen's words only increased his rage. He used a devastating combination of water and wind, creating a dark tornado that bore down on Kaen with destructive force.

Kaen, with the power of fire, earth and light, countered the attack with a glowing barrier. The collision of opposing energies created an explosion that shook the entire island, toppling trees and fragmenting the ground. In the midst of the chaos, Kaen continued to see fragments of the past, remembering Fen's humanity and feeling the urgency to save him.

Flashback:

In their first meeting, Kaen had offered Fen the chance to seek answers together, but circumstances led them to a confrontation. Despite this, Kaen had never forgotten the purity of Fen's quest, his desire for justice and truth.

Back in reality, Kaen realized that he had to do more than defend himself. He had to find a way to get to Fen, to get him out of the darkness before it was too late. With renewed determination, Kaen redoubled his efforts, using the combined power of the three dragons not only to counter Fen's attacks, but also to create openings, moments in which he could speak to her, reach for her heart.

"Fen," Kaen shouted once more, "this is not you. Don't let the darkness consume you. Remember who you were, what you were fighting for."

Fen, however briefly, seemed to falter, his gaze lost somewhere between the present and the past. But fury and darkness took control again, and the battle continued, fiercer than ever. Kaen knew that time was running out, and he must find a way to break the barrier of rage and despair that enveloped Fen, before they both destroyed each other and, with them, everything they once loved.

The fighting continued with increasing intensity. Kaen, seeing the brief doubt in Fen's eyes, realized that he could no longer try to save him with words alone. He had to face it with all the strength he possessed, hoping to bring Fen back to his senses. Fen's attacks became increasingly aggressive and uncontrolled, as the darkness consumed him deeper.

Kaen, with the experience of a warrior hardened by a thousand battles, began to notice a pattern in Fen's attacks. Every time Fen launched an attack, he completely neglected his defense. Taking advantage of this weakness, Kaen focused on skillfully dodging Fen's attacks, looking for the perfect moment to counterattack.

With a clear strategy in mind, Kaen began to accumulate the power of the three dragons within him. As he dodged Fen's attacks, the aura of fire, earth, and light around Kaen intensified, forming a glow that illuminated the battlefield.

Finally, Kaen saw the opening he had been waiting for. With a quick and precise movement, he released a powerful blast of energy directly towards Fen. The shockwave enveloped Fen, hitting him with overwhelming force and breaking, however momentarily, the hold of darkness over him.

In that brief moment of clarity, Fen stopped, showing signs of confusion and deep pain. His eyes, normally filled with fury, now reflected suffering and internal struggle. He seemed to be on the verge of surrender, but also on the verge of desperation.

Kaen took advantage of that moment. He extended his hand toward Fen, his voice firm but laden with empathy. "Fen, that's enough. You don't have to continue down this path. You can still save yourself, we can still find the truth and the justice you seek, but you need to get out of the darkness. Take my hand and together we can stop this madness."

Fen looked at Kaen's outstretched hand, his eyes filled with uncertainty. Silence fell over the battlefield for an instant, as the energies of the dragons collided and resonated in the air. Fen was at a crossroads, caught between the desire to continue his revenge and the possibility of finding redemption.

Kaen kept his hand outstretched, his gaze steady and filled with compassion. He knew that this was a crucial moment, one that could define not only Fen's destiny, but that of the entire world. Hope glimmered on the horizon, a hope that even in the deepest darkness, there was always a chance for redemption.

As Fen hesitated, the battlefield remained in a tense silence. The decision he made at that moment could change the course of history.

Fen looked at Kaen's outstretched hand, his eyes filled with internal struggle. It looked like, for a brief moment, he was going to accept the offer of redemption. However, just before his fingers touched Kaen's hand, darkness possessed him once more. This time, it wasn't the uncontrolled anger he had shown before. Now, Fen was surrounded by a murderous aura and an eerie calm.

With impressive speed, Fen dashed towards Kaen. In the blink of an eye, he dealt a devastating blow, concentrating multiple elements into an attack that surpassed anything Kaen had seen before. The impact pushed Kaen with overwhelming force, severely injuring him despite the earth armor he had managed to conjure at the last second.

Kaen felt the pain and weight of the attack. Fen's intensity had reached a new level, one that seemed unstoppable. As he stood up, his body protesting the effort, Kaen realized that the situation had changed drastically. He was no longer sure he could save Fen without having to end her life.

With a mix of anguish and determination, Kaen prepared for the next phase of the battle. He knew he must use all his power, all the strength he had received from the dragons, to stop Fen once and for all. Hope for redemption for his former rival was fading, replaced by the need to end the threat he posed.

Kaen closed his eyes for a moment, concentrating deeply. The power of fire, earth, and light intertwined within him, forming a formidable force. With a look of resolve, Kaen threw himself back into the fight, determined to use every ounce of his power to end the fight.

Fen, now completely consumed by darkness, attacked with a precision and lethality that Kaen could barely counter. Fen's every move was filled with killing intent, and his speed made dodging and defending an almost impossible task.

The battlefield became a spectacle of pure destruction. Fen's attacks disintegrated everything in their path, while Kaen used his control over the elements to counter and attack in a desperate attempt to gain ground. Shockwaves from her powers shook the surroundings, each impact echoing like thunder across the desolate island that was once Fen's home.

Kaen knew that this battle could not last forever. He had to find a way to stop Fen, to free the man trapped inside that murderous darkness. But every time he launched an attack, Fen seemed to respond with even greater strength, a power that seemed to feed on his own desperation and fury.

With every blow, every explosion of energy, Kaen realized that the end was near. The battle, at its climax, would become the outcome of a story marked by tragedy, revenge and sacrifice. With one last look into Fen's eyes, Kaen prepared to do whatever it took to end this fight, even if it meant sacrificing his own life in the process.

The island trembled under the weight of their confrontation, and the fate of the world balanced precariously on the shoulders of these two warriors.

The battle between Kaen and Fen did not only affect the island on which they fought. Its impacts resonated throughout the realms, wreaking havoc and wreaking havoc. Every attack unleashed, every burst of power, sent waves of destruction that disrupted the stability of the entire world.

In the **Kingdom of Water**, the epicenter of the battle, the tribes and inhabitants lived in constant fear. The seas churned violently, creating tsunamis that devastated the coasts. Structures were collapsing, and coastal cities were beginning to disappear beneath the raging waves. The inhabitants took shelter as best they could, but Fen's power, amplified by the darkness, seemed unstoppable. The very forces that sustained life in the kingdom were turning against them, threatening to annihilate everything they once knew.

In the **Kingdom of Fire**, the earth trembled under the feet of its inhabitants. The normally contained volcanoes were beginning to show signs of dangerous activity. Fissures in the earth spewed fire and ash, creating an apocalyptic atmosphere. The inhabitants, remembering the ancient legends of dragons and their battles, feared that their world was coming to an end.

The **Kingdom of Earth** also suffered the consequences. Earthquakes shook the mountains and valleys, destabilizing the terrain. Crops were destroyed and infrastructure collapsed. Panic spread among the people, who sought refuge in caves and underground fortresses, fearful that the fury of the dragons could reach them.

Even the **Kingdom of Air**, high in its peaks and normally far from the terrestrial tumult, felt the effects of the battle. Wind currents became erratic and dangerous, making navigation and communication impossible. Villages in the mountains battled sudden and destructive storms, while wise men desperately searched for a solution to the crisis.

In the **Kingdom of Light**, normally a bastion of peace and serenity, the skies were darkening. The guardians of the kingdom, enlightened beings, felt a deep disturbance. The sacred temples vibrated with discordant energy, and the priests led by Luminara prayed fervently for divine intervention that could stop the catastrophe. However, without the power of "The Glorious One", who now resided in Kaen, they felt vulnerable and unprotected.

The **Realm of Darkness**, a place of mystery and secrets, was also affected. The shadows seemed to come to life, and the inhabitants, accustomed to the darkness, were in a state of anxiety. The leaders of the dark sects, such as Noctis, watched the growing imbalance with concern, aware that even their kingdom was in danger. Without "The Dark One", who was now part of Fen, there was no guide to handling the crisis.

Back on **Battle Island**Kaen and Fen continued to clash with inhuman intensity. The energy unleashed by both combatants continued to increase, taking the destruction to an unimaginable level. The ground beneath their feet was constantly fragmenting and reforming, as if nature itself was reacting to their struggle.

Kaen, with the experience and wisdom accumulated throughout his life and his recent fusions with dragons, was constantly searching for a way to break the darkness that controlled Fen. But each attempt seemed futile in the face of the relentless fury of Fen, who was completely immersed in his rage and uncontrolled power.

The island, once a place of happy memories for Fen, was becoming a field of ruins. Memories of his family and his previous life were swallowed up by the destruction that now surrounded him. And as the battle intensified, Kaen realized that the price of this contest could be the total destruction, not only of the island, but of all the kingdoms.

As Kaen dodged another devastating attack from Fen, his thoughts turned to the people of the kingdoms. He knew he had to put an end to this, not only to save Fen, but to prevent a global catastrophe. Determination burned in his heart like the fire within him, and with a cry of defiance, he prepared for the next assault.

The fate of the world hung in the balance, and the resolution of this battle would define the future of all kingdoms. Hope and fear intertwined in the hearts of all beings, as Kaen and Fen faced each other in a battle that would decide the fate of all they knew.

And so, amidst the chaos and destruction, the fight continued, with the fate of Fen, Kaen, and the entire world hanging in the balance.

Chapter XVII: The Climax of the Battle

The fight between Kaen and Fen continued with unimaginable ferocity. Both warriors, now masters of their respective elements, unleashed all their power without restraint, creating a scene of total destruction around them. The clash of water against earth, light against darkness and wind against fire generated a heartbreaking chaos that was felt in every corner of the world.

Kaen, with the combined strength of the fire, earth and light dragons, launched devastating attacks. His blows were precise and his defense impenetrable. Every time Fen lunged at him with his dark fury, Kaen responded with a counterattack that lit up the sky with flashes of pure light and volcanic explosions.

For his part, Fen, consumed by darkness and rage, used the power of water, wind and darkness with impressive skill. Their movements were swift and deadly, sending out razor-sharp gusts of wind, and columns of water rising like tsunamis, only to be instantly turned to ice and launched like projectiles. The darkness that enveloped him seemed to absorb the light around him, creating an intimidating and destructive aura.

The battlefield, once a serene island, was now a shattered terrain. The seas churned furiously, the mountains crumbled, and the sky darkened with the energy of the conflicting elements. Fen, in his insane state, did not seem to notice the destruction of his former home. His only intention was to destroy Kaen and anything that stood in his way.

Kaen, in contrast, struggled with a mix of sadness and determination. He remembered the man Fen used to be, a warrior in search of truth and justice, not this creature consumed by revenge and darkness. Each attack from Kaen was not only an attempt to stop Fen, but also to save him from the darkness that devoured him.

The mastery of both warriors in their elements was evident. Kaen used his control over the earth to build defensive walls and hurl incandescent rocks. His mastery of fire created storms of flame that devastated everything in its path, while the light emanating from it offered blinding flashes that confused Fen.

Fen, in turn, responded with equally formidable force. He used wind to deflect Kaen's attacks, water to smother flames, and darkness to absorb light. His attacks were savage but calculated, aimed with deadly precision that kept Kaen in constant motion.

The intensity of the battle reached its climax. The attacks of both combatants became faster and more powerful, each trying to surpass the other. The ground shook with each impact, and the air vibrated with the energy released. It seemed that the world itself was on the verge of breaking apart.

As the two warriors continued their fight, the fate of the kingdoms hung in the balance. The battle between Kaen and Fen was not just a confrontation between two powerful beings, but a confrontation that would decide the future of everything that existed. Hope, desperation, courage and fury were intertwined in every movement, every blow, every cry of defiance.

And so, at the climax of the battle, Kaen and Fen gave their all, showing total mastery of their elements, fighting not only for their lives, but for the fate of a world that watched, helplessly, as this epic confrontation unfolded. .

In the midst of the brutal battle, as Kaen and Fen's powers clashed again and again, something peculiar began to happen. For brief moments, the darkness surrounding Fen seemed to fade. In those fleeting moments, his fury dissipated and Fen was once again the man he once was, free of the madness that controlled him.

These flashes of clarity were as fleeting as they were hopeful. In the midst of a ferocious attack, Fen's eyes softened, and for a brief second, he seemed to recognize Kaen not as an enemy, but as someone with whom he shared a greater purpose. However, as soon as these moments arrived, they were suppressed by the darkness that consumed him, returning him to his state of destructive frenzy.

Kaen, focused on the battle, could not perceive these momentary changes in Fen. To him, Fen remained an implacable threat, whose uncontrolled fury endangered not only him, but everyone. Each clash of powers between them generated waves of energy that shook the earth, air and sea. The elements raged around them, reflecting the intensity of their confrontation.

Despite Kaen's efforts to find an opening and reach the true Fen, the fight continued. Fen's moments of clarity were so brief that they did not alter the pace of the battle. Kaen continued to launch combined attacks of fire, earth, and light, attempting to disarm Fen and protect himself from his relentless assault of water, wind, and darkness.

In one of those brief moments, Fen seemed to stop, his gaze lost in space. It was as if he was fighting internally against the darkness that dominated him. But before Kaen could react, the fury returned, and Fen resumed his attack with renewed aggression.

The destruction around him knew no limits. The island, Fen's former home, was unrecognizable. What was once a place of peace and happiness had become a devastated battlefield. The waves rose like liquid walls, the winds howled like unleashed beasts, and the earth trembled beneath their feet. Nature itself seemed to scream in agony at the violence that was unfolding.

Every moment of clarity Fen experienced was a reminder of the person he once was. These moments, although brief, gave hope that there was still a part of Fen that was struggling to free itself from the darkness. However, the battle continued unabated, with Kaen and Fen surrendering completely to their powers in a confrontation that seemed to have no end.

The fight continued, and with each clash of its elements, the world teetered on the brink of destruction. Kaen, unaware of Fen's moments of clarity, remained steadfast in his determination to stop him, hoping that somewhere within that uncontrolled fury there was still something of the true Fen left.

And so the battle raged on, with glimmers of hope interspersed between the fury and devastation. Kaen and Fen continued to face each other, each doing their best, not knowing that in those brief moments of clarity, the fate of the world could be slowly changing.

The battle between Kaen and Fen reached its climax when both warriors decided to charge up their most powerful attacks, combining all the elements they controlled. Fen channeled water, wind, and darkness, while Kaen summoned fire, earth, and light. The skies darkened and the ground shook as both attacks collided, creating an earth-shaking explosion of energy.

The resulting shockwave was so powerful that it launched Kaen and Fen in opposite directions, throwing them across the devastated island. The explosion resonated throughout the entire world, wreaking havoc on every kingdom and leaving both warriors completely unconscious.

An instant later, Fen was the first to regain consciousness. Opening his eyes, he found the world around him in ruins and his mind engulfed in confusion. He could barely remember recent events, but one thing was clear: he had been in a fierce battle with Kaen.

Disoriented, Fen staggered to his feet and saw Kaen lying motionless on the ground. At that moment, his mind focused on a single goal: to end the battle once and for all. He approached Kaen with the intention of attacking and putting an end to everything.

However, when he tried to summon the power of the dragons, he discovered to his surprise that he could no longer sense their presence. Perhaps because of extreme fatigue, or perhaps because the essence of the dragons had faded, Fen realized that he was alone with his human strength. This moment of bewilderment gave Kaen enough time to wake up.

Kaen opened his eyes and found himself in a state similar to Fen: without the powers of the dragons and feeling only his own human strength. He stood up slowly, pained but determined, and saw Fen standing a few meters away, equally stripped of his supernatural abilities.

They both looked at each other, realizing that the situation had changed drastically. They were no longer warriors imbued with the power of dragons, but simple men facing each other on a desolate battlefield. The devastation around them was a testament to the ferocity of their fight and the enormous power they had both possessed.

The silence that followed the explosion was almost deafening. Fen, still recovering from the confusion, slowly lowered the hand he had raised to attack. Kaen, with a look of determination and exhaustion, understood that this was an opportunity to change the course of their confrontation.

With the dragons' powers vanished, the fate of the world and themselves now depended on their own human decisions and abilities. At that moment, both prepared to face the new reality that awaited them, without knowing exactly how this final battle would end.

Without the dragons' powers, the battle between Kaen and Fen was reduced to a fight of human strength and skill. Fury and desperation still burned in Fen's eyes, as Kaen, with his greater experience as a warrior, quickly took the lead. His strikes were precise and calculated, taking advantage of every opening in Fen's defense.

Kaen moved with the grace of a seasoned combatant, and each of his attacks weakened Fen, who, despite his determination, could not match his opponent's tactical skill. Blow after blow, Kaen managed to corner Fen, finally leaving him on his knees on the ground.

The air was thick with tension. Kaen, breathing heavily but with unwavering firmness, raised his sword, ready to deliver the final blow. However, instead of attacking, he lowered his sword and addressed Fen with a voice filled with conviction and hope.

"Fen, I know deep down you're still searching for answers about what happened to your family," Kaen said, his words echoing in the silence around them. "Together, we can be the bannermen of the new world to come. It doesn't have to end like this. There is a way to resolve this without more destruction."

Tears began to roll down Fen's cheeks, his eyes showing a glimpse of the person he once was, before being consumed by darkness and fury. Kaen's words reached his heart, and for a moment, it seemed that Fen was willing to accept the offer of peace.

However, at the last second, in an impulsive and desperate movement, Fen gritted his teeth and, with a cry of pain and rage, pierced Kaen's chest with his sword. Blood gushed from Kaen's body, who, surprised, staggered a step back.

Kaen, with a look of disbelief and sadness, fell to the ground, feeling the life escape from his body. Fen, still with tears in his eyes, dropped his sword, falling to his knees next to Kaen, overcome by a mix of emotions.

"I'm sorry… I couldn't… I couldn't stop," Fen whispered, her voice breaking from crying.

Kaen, with his last strength, raised a hand and placed it on Fen's shoulder. "Still...there is still hope, Fen. Don't let all of this be in vain," he drawled before his eyes slowly closed.

The battlefield fell into a dead silence, with Fen kneeling next to Kaen's body, feeling the weight of his actions and the pain of loss. The battle was over, but the consequences of his actions were just beginning to become apparent.

With tears streaming down her cheeks and her sword still buried in Kaen's chest, Fen spoke, her voice shaking with a mix of pain and fury. "Kaen... I never wanted it to end like this. The truth... I discovered it before this battle began. Everything that happened, the meteor that destroyed my home and murdered my family, was an illusion created by "The Pacific"."

Kaen, with pain visible on his face and his breath slowing, listened attentively as Fen continued. "He manipulated everything to break the pact between the dragons and start a war between the nations. I was deceived, controlled by the Water Dragon, and when I finally realized it, the fury I felt was more than I had ever known."

Fen paused, his voice breaking under the weight of his emotions. "That fury... was what allowed me to expel "The Pacific" from my body and put an end to it. But that same fury was what left me vulnerable to the darkness. I let myself be consumed by it because I no longer knew what to believe, who to trust."

Kaen, with an effort, raised his hand and placed it on Fen's, his eyes filled with understanding and compassion. "Fen... I understood your pain. I always did," he murmured, his words barely audible.

Fen leaned forward, his tears falling onto Kaen's face. "I'm sorry, Kaen. I'm sorry I was so blind. I'm sorry I hurt you. But now, without the power of the dragons, I don't know how to fix all this. I don't know how to bring peace to such a broken world."

Kaen squeezed Fen's hand lightly, his voice weakening but still firm. "There is... there is always hope, Fen. You can... you can find a way. Don't let... the darkness consume you again. Use... use your pain to build a better future."

With those last words, Kaen closed his eyes, his body finally succumbing to his injuries. Fen, still on his knees, let out an anguished cry that echoed across the empty battlefield. The truth he had discovered weighed heavily on him, but it also gave him a new perspective.

The illusion created by "The Pacific" had triggered a series of events that led to destruction and war. Now, with Kaen dead and the darkness still latent within him, Fen knew he must find a way to redeem himself and make amends for the damage done. The battle was over, but the real challenge was just beginning.

Fen, slowly rising, pulled the sword from Kaen's body and stabbed it into the ground beside him. He looked up at the sky, determination in his eyes, and swore that he would find a way to restore balance and bring the peace they longed for. Not only to honor the memory of Kaen, but also to fulfill the legacy of the dragons and save the world from chaos.

Fen, standing in the midst of the devastation, knelt next to Kaen's limp body. Her tears fell silently, mixing with the blood and dirt that covered the battlefield. "I'm sorry, Kaen," he whispered with deep regret, his voice shaking. "I should never have allowed the darkness to control me. But now, with this new determination, I know I can control it."

He slowly stood up, and with renewed determination, took up his sword. Darkness began to flow from the handle to the tip, enveloping her in a sinister aura. Fen knew what he had to do. It was a necessary, if heartbreaking, act. He plunged the sword into Kaen's body again, this time completely imbuing her with darkness.

As he did so, he felt Kaen's essence, along with the powers of the three dragons that lived within him, begin to flow into him. It was an immense, overwhelming power, but Fen was determined to control it. He knew that with this power, he could repair the damage done and bring a needed balance to the world.

Kaen's body began to slowly fade away, his essence being absorbed by Fen's sword. Every particle, every fragment of energy was integrated into Fen, increasing its power and wisdom. Kaen's figure disappeared completely, leaving Fen alone, alone and surrounded by destruction.

The battlefield, once a place of happy memories for Fen, was now a wasteland of ruins and despair. Fen stood there, holding his sword, feeling the weight of the lives he had taken and the power he had gained. But he also felt the responsibility that now fell on him.

With the power of the dragons and the wisdom of Kaen, Fen knew he had the ability to change the course of the world. But first, he had to redeem himself. He had to find a way to restore the much-needed peace and balance.

"Kaen," he murmured, looking up at the sky. "I promise that I will use this power to bring peace. I will not allow your sacrifice to be in vain. I will not let the world fall into darkness."

With that promise in his heart, Fen began to walk away from the destruction and toward an uncertain future. He knew that the road would be long and difficult, but he was determined to fulfill his purpose. The dragons were gone, but their legacy lived on, and with that, the world still had hope.

Away from the battlefield, Fen walked in silence, his mind in a storm of thoughts and emotions. The destruction he had left behind weighed on him like an overwhelming burden. He wondered what steps he should take, how he could fulfill his promise to Kaen and restore balance to such a fractured world.

Suddenly, a voice echoed inside him. It was the voice of the Dragon of Darkness. "Fen," the voice began, soft but piercing.

"There is much you should know. Things that you do not know and that have been hidden from you."

Fen stopped, listening carefully. The dragon's voice continued. "First, you should know that "The Pacific" planned to break the ancient pact that the dragons had to maintain the balance of the world. His ambition led him to manipulate events and people, including you, to trigger a war between the nations."

Fen already knew that he had been used by "The Pacific", but discovering the extent of his manipulation left him perplexed. "And you," he said with a trembling voice, "did you use me too?"

The Dragon of Darkness responded with solemn calm. "I knew how to control your body. It was a decision I made to make sure you could put an end to all of this. It wasn't easy, but I believed it was necessary to stop "The Pacific" and restore balance."

The revelation hit Fen like a blow, but he did not give in to anger. I knew I had to listen to the end. The dragon's voice continued. "The Pacific" and "The Changeling" met before the fight you had with Kaen and "The Firm One". It was in that meeting that "The Pacific" took control of your body for the first time to kill "The Changeling" and absorb his essence, at the same time it was that I learned how to do it myself."

The Dragon of Darkness continued, "After the battle, Kaen made a pact with "The Firm One" and "The Glorious One". This pact was for Kaen to rule the world, carrying the power of all the dragons within him. That is why so much the Dragon of the Earth and the Dragon of Light sacrificed themselves to grant him their powers."

Fen closed his eyes, feeling the sadness and regret in the dragon's words. "I'm sorry, Fen," the dragon continued. "I took control of your body because I believed it was the only way to put an end to all of this. I knew it must disappear, just as "The Wild One" had predicted. It was time for dragons to no longer exist in this world."

At these words, Fen was stunned. The Dragon of Darkness materialized in front of him, its imposing form shrouded in shadows. "Now I leave the rest to you," said the dragon. "I trust that you will be able to restore balance and peace throughout the world."

With a final breath, the Dragon of Darkness began to fade away, giving all of its essence and power to Fen. Dark energy flowed towards him, filling him with indescribable strength. Fen felt a mixture of gratitude and sadness as the dragon completely disappeared.

"Thank you," Fen murmured, his words filled with emotion. "I won't let you down."

With the new strength of the Dragon of Darkness within him, Fen felt more determined than ever. I knew the road would be arduous and full of challenges, but I was ready to face them. The fate of the world was in his hands, and he was determined to fulfill his purpose: restore peace and balance to a world that so needed it.

Fen, now charged with the power and wisdom of all dragons, knew that his destiny had been changed forever. He felt an immense responsibility on his shoulders, one that he could not ignore. Remembering the tragedies he had experienced and the sacrifices that had been made, he made a firm decision: he would become the guardian of the land.

I knew it wouldn't be an easy task. Distrust and fear had taken deep root in the hearts of the people. Fen would have to earn their trust and prove that he was capable of uniting them under one kingdom, using the powers of the dragons to bring prosperity and balance to a devastated world.

With this new resolution, Fen set his first goal: to recover completely and learn to control the immense powers he now carried within him. He retreated to a secluded place, where he could train and meditate in peace, away from the chaos he had left behind.

Days turned into weeks, and weeks into months. During this time, Fen dedicated himself to understanding each of the powers he possessed. He learned to dominate the fire of "The Wild One", to control the earth of "The Firm One", to manage the light of "The Glorious one", to flow with the water of "The Pacific", to cross the skies with the wind of "The Changeling" and to understand the depth of darkness he had received from the Dragon of Darkness.

Each workout was one step closer to his goal. Fen felt himself getting stronger, not only physically, but mentally as well. The fusion of so many different powers and essences had changed him profoundly, but he was determined to use this new strength for good.

The months turned into years. Fen trained tirelessly, day and night, in various environments and conditions. He spent long periods in each of the elements, completely submerging himself in the water to feel the calm and strength of the sea, facing wind storms to understand the freedom and chaos of the air, and immersing himself in the most absolute darkness to embrace and control the power of the Dragon of Darkness.

During winters, he braved freezing temperatures and used internal fire to stay warm and active. In the summers, he endured the scorching heat and pressure of the sun, learning to channel the light at its maximum intensity. During the autumns and springs, he merged with the earth, feeling the change and renewal these seasons brought.

Throughout these years, Fen not only learned to master his powers, but also discovered a new understanding of himself and the world around him. His skills were honed, and his mind became clearer. The wisdom of the dragons became an intrinsic part of his being, guiding him every step he took.

Finally, after years of training and self-discovery, Fen felt he was ready. He had achieved an internal balance and a mastery of his powers that gave him the confidence to face any challenge. He knew that the next step would be the most difficult: unifying the kingdoms and bringing a new era of peace and prosperity to the world.

Thus, Fen prepared to resume his mission. I knew the road would be long and full of obstacles, but I was ready to face them. Determined to protect and rule wisely, Fen moved toward his ultimate destiny: to unify all the kingdoms and bring a new era of peace and prosperity to the world.

The world had changed irrevocably since the beginning of Fen's journey. Remembering the pain and loss that had driven him on his quest for revenge, he now understood that those same feelings had been transformed into a greater mission: to bring peace and unity to a fragmented world.

From the moment Fen lost his family due to the illusion created by "The Pacific", his life had been a series of trials and battles. Every encounter, every fusion with the dragons, and every confrontation had brought him closer to his purpose. The fight with Kaen, who was once his enemy and then an ally on the path to the truth, was a turning point. Kaen had understood the need to unify the powers of the dragons and had sacrificed his life to grant that power to Fen.

With the power of all the dragons within him, Fen had retreated to train and master his abilities. Over the years, he became a master of each element, learning not only to control, but to harmonize the powers of fire, earth, water, wind, light and darkness.

Fen remembered each step of his journey: the initial confrontation with Kaen, the betrayal and manipulation of "The Pacific", the truth revealed by "The Dark One" and the sacrifices of "The Firm One" and "The Glorious one". Everything he had experienced had prepared him for the moment he now faced.

The world, during his absence, had experienced chaos and destruction, but also hope and renewal. Kingdoms teetered between fear and hope, waiting for a leader who could guide them to a brighter future. Fen knew he was that leader, although the task would be monumental. Unifying the kingdoms and restoring balance would be their greatest challenge, but also their destiny.

The sun was beginning to rise on the horizon, illuminating the new day with a warm, golden light. Fen stood up, his figure silhouetted against the dawn. With the weight of his past and the promise of a better future, he walked towards the horizon. His steps were firm, and his determination was unwavering.

Fen's journey was not over; in fact, it was just beginning. The peace he sought would not be easy to achieve, and the challenges to come would be great. But with the power and wisdom of the dragons within him, and with the strength he had gained through his trials, Fen was ready to face any challenge that came his way.

The world awaited his arrival, and Fen, with a heart full of hope and new resolve, headed toward his final destination. Fen's story was not over; a new chapter was about to begin. And as he moved toward the horizon, the future unfolded before him, full of possibilities and promises of a better tomorrow.